THIS
IS THE
AFTERLIFE

Stories

JEFF CHON

Sagging
Meniscus

These stories have previously appeared in the following publications: "P.A.LA.D.I.N." in *The North American Review*; "Tanuki" in *Blunderbuss*; "All These Lives" in *Disclaimer*; "Stay Put" in *Word Riot*; "There's No Connection Here" in *King Ludd's Rag*; "This is Not Happening" in *Fiddleblack*; "I'll Allow It, Maybe Just This Once" in *Okay Donkey* and *The Best Small Fictions 2021*; "Not a Fever, Not a Dream" in *Excuse Me*; "Undead" in *Red Fez*; "This Is the Afterlife" in *Juked*.

I'd like to express my gratitude to the editors and readers at each and every one of these amazing publications. This book wouldn't exist were it not for your support and generosity.

Set in Williams Caslon Text with LaTeX.

ISBN: 978-1-952386-45-9 (paperback)
ISBN: 978-1-952386-46-6 (ebook)
Library of Congress Control Number: 2022941553

Sagging Meniscus Press
Montclair, New Jersey
saggingmeniscus.com

As always, for Dina, Mia, and Avery

CONTENTS

THIS IS THE AFTERLIFE

P.A.L.A.D.I.N.

WE STARE at the mound of record sleeves—me, Wave, and Darcy—piled high on the lawn, across the street from the courthouse: Judas Priest, Iron Maiden, Megadeth—someone has even thrown in Genesis and Pat Benatar for some reason—and I remember the filmstrip from Mr. Dornan's history class, the one with the footage of Nazis burning all those books they'd deemed un-German. I remember Mr. Dornan, who'd served two tours in Vietnam, telling us this was what separated America from the Communists. And here's Mr. Dornan, now flipping his daughter's Cinderella and Mötley Crüe records onto the pile like playing cards. Stephanie Dornan begs him to stop, and mascara inks down her cheeks as her father tosses the records one by one with dramatic effect. Wave and Darcy cover their mouths and snicker as Stephanie collapses tearfully onto the lawn. Mr. Dornan glares at them—and he's right to do so, at least right now. He's never liked Wave or Darcy, and they didn't like him much either. He once even tried to have Darcy expelled for wearing her *Holiday in Cambodia* T-shirt to school, telling her Cambodia was no holiday, that maybe she should try talking to people who'd sacrificed their youth for the privilege of getting spit on by people like her. None of this makes any sense—I guess it makes sense in a sick, twisted sort of way, but things shouldn't make sense in that way.

They just shouldn't.

Then Mr. Dornan looks at me, and I turn away. Back when Mr. Dornan was Coach Dornan, and I was the 145-pounder on his wrestling team, we'd gotten along well enough, but he'd gone one Gook too far, and no amount of apologies, no amount of *I wasn't talking about you*'s could put us back together again. I'd told him Gook was short for *hanguk*, which means Korea, so he actually was talking about me. And then Coach Dornan tried to assure me he was only talking about the VC sappers that had tried to kill him and his friends, the ones who'd taken his brother in '71. And I told him I didn't care about his brother, but I didn't mean it—I didn't not care about his brother—but that was that. He did ask me to not burn this bridge, but how could either of us go back at that point?

Mrs. Dornan helps Stephanie to her feet, reaches out to wipe away the tears. But Stephanie pulls away, runs off, the fringes of her leather jacket flopping with each stride. Her records slide off the pile and onto the grass. Mr. Dornan tries to push them back onto the pile with his feet, but they keep sliding back. A cowboy in a blue, short-sleeved shirt and red tie picks up Stephanie's record sleeves and tosses them back into the pile, douses them with lighter fluid until they stick. Mr. Dornan watches Stephanie run into the arms of her denim-clad heavy metal friends. He shakes his head. Darcy hits my shoulder with the back of her hand.

Jesus Christ, she says. You're like a puppy dog. Let it go. You're totally not her type.

Pastor Mike hugs a megaphone to his fat chest while speaking to the reporter from Channel 7 News. The place is crawling with reporters. Kurt Loder has even shown up with an MTV News Crew, which is why Darcy's wearing her *Bela Lugosi's Dead* T-shirt—it was important to her that MTV knew we weren't all small-town Bible-thumpers, that some of us actually listened to real music. The Bible-thumpers mill about—most of them out-of-towners—and Wave takes a swig of stolen Amaretto from a flask and then shoves it back into his jacket.

Six days ago, Hiro Nishihara tried to hang himself in his basement. It was on a Monday. When Mr. Simon broke the news during pre-Calculus, everyone looked at me, and I knew it was because I was the only other Oriental dude in the class. The Fang sisters were there too, but no one associated them with the likes of me or Hiro because they were on Prom Committee, and Student Council, and fogged up rear windows at the drive-in. Hiro's a Japanese metalhead, and I'm a Korean kid who wishes he was David Gahan, and in this stupid hick town, being a Korean kid who likes Depeche Mode is like having a Kick Me sign stitched on the back of every shirt. The way they all looked at me in class that day—even Doris Fang, who shook her head and then turned away, as if to remind me she was nothing like me—kind of made me miss the protection my letterman's jacket used to provide.

According to the metal kids, Hiro had looped a bedsheet over the wooden beam in his basement and tied it around his neck. *A Cleansing Fire* by Paladin, his favorite album from his favorite band, was blaring from the woodgrain HiFi he'd gotten on his eleventh birthday. He and I used to spend a lot of time in that basement way back when—before Hiro became a metalhead and before I became whatever I became—playing *D&D*. We had no other friends, so he was both Dungeon Master and Magic-User, and I played the Fighter and Thief characters.

Sometimes, due to the exhaustion of playing a long campaign wearing all those hats, we'd ride our bikes to the bowling alley and hide in the arcade, hoping the bigger kids wouldn't notice us. That was five years ago—it all seemed so much simpler then. It's silly for me to say that—that life was simpler then. Shit, I'm only seventeen years old—how complicated is my life, really?

I always tell myself the past only seems simpler because I've had time to process it. The only thing I can do right now is react, which only makes the future that much scarier. But as unsure as I am of the present, as much as I dread the future, thinking of the past still fills me with this sense of sadness I can't quite wrap my head around. The closest I come is to call it homesickness, and even that doesn't seem right. The only thing that makes me feel better is to look back on those days and tell myself, Man, life seemed so much simpler back then, as if I somehow know better now.

A group of middle-aged women come forward, each holding a stack of records against their chests. Every time one of them tosses records onto the pile, the others cross themselves and gaze at the sky as if they're offering those Ozzy and Dokken records to God himself.

Hiro's father came over the night after he'd tried to hang himself. I sat on the stairs and listened to Dr. Nishihara, the town dentist, tell my dad how he'd come home because some little kid puked all over his shoes and he needed to change, how he'd heard music blaring from the basement and was ready to kill Hiro for cutting school. He broke down in tears four times and I hated myself for eavesdropping.

Word got around Hiro was listening to Paladin when he tried to hang himself, so Pastor Mike called the other churches in the area and asked them to help stage a protest against what he'd always called The Devil's Music, asking them to bring every heavy metal record they could get their hands on so they could stage a burning. It made headlines all over the country, which is why Kurt Loder is here. Eoin Brannigan, the lead singer of Paladin, even went on *Nightline*, telling Ted Koppel his music was a celebration of life, not death, not evil. I felt sorry for Brannigan with his ponytail, and dark glasses, and crooked tie. I hear Pastor Mike might even run for Congress because of all this, as if anyone would vote for that hypocrite. Hiro is now at the hospital, lying in a coma, and no matter how many times my parents yell at me, I can't bring myself to go and see him.

I do feel bad about ditching Hiro, but it wasn't like he didn't play a part in all of this. At the beginning of junior high, I'd asked him to join the wrestling team with me, so we could stop getting picked on. It would've been perfect, and he would've finally fit in—the team actually needed a 103-pounder—but he said something about jocks being dumb and all sorts of other crap that, honestly, turned out to be true. But I did try.

People eventually stopped calling me Chink by the beginning of eighth grade—well some of them anyway—and Hiro slowly began to hang out with Bryan Mayfield, and Stephanie Dornan, and the other metal kids, growing his hair out, wearing ripped jeans, smoking on the other side of the parking lot. He'd even begun playing bass, he and Bryan starting a band called Balrog, which my dumb jock buddies called Ballrub even though I'd pull them aside and ask them to knock it off every time they did it. Hiro would stare at me and just shake his head, the iron-on patch across the back of his jacket, featuring Paladin's Undead Knight mascot, growing smaller and smaller as he walked away from me and the snickering dicks I used to hang out with.

Wave takes another gulp of Amaretto, and Darcy asks if we thought Kurt Loder might want to interview us, and I tell her I don't know. Pastor Mike talks to an old lady on a walker. She points over at the metalheads who've come down to heckle them, and she and Pastor Mike shake their heads. Bryan Mayfield—lead singer of Balrog, aka Ballrub—asks the old lady what she's pointing at, tells her and Pastor Mike they should be ashamed of themselves, that Hiro was his friend, and they should have the fucking decency not to use him for their stupid cause. An out-of-towner tells Bryan to watch his mouth, and then Bryan tells him to fuck off, and the out-of-towner calls Bryan a piece of white trash.

I haven't thought it until now, but for the most part, the metal kids actually were white trash. Other than Hiro and Stephanie, most of these kids literally lived on the other side of the tracks, where the old shoe factory stood, abandoned since I was in preschool. Pastor Mike walks around shaking hands and hugging the out-of-towners. He stands, and laughs, and slaps their backs like this is all some game. Maybe this is all some game. Maybe he doesn't believe any of the crap he's saying. It wouldn't surprise me at all if he didn't believe.

Three weeks ago, Wave, Darcy, and I piled into Wave's Granada and drove into the city to buy records and goof around. We'd stopped at a gas station to fill up for the drive home, and Darcy went inside to get a Pepsi, and pay for the gas. She ran out almost immediately and told us to hide in the car. She told us to keep our heads down, but Wave decided to take a look.

Hi Pastor Mike, he shouted.

He squinted over in our direction and then began walking toward the Granada, holding a brown paper bag.

David, he said, is that you?

It's me, Wave said.

Who's that in there with you? Hiya, Darcy. Hello, Wesley.

Hi, Pastor Mike.

Just getting some gas, he said. And a few essentials for the drive home. You know, junk food and what have you. Don't tell the Missus you saw this.

We all laughed—Darcy laughed harder than we did—and told him his secret was safe with us. It wasn't until he drove away that Darcy told us she'd run out because she'd seen him at the counter buying porno mags.

Actual porno mags, she'd said. The nasty stuff like *Hustler*, and *Cheri*, and some other one I couldn't see—the same dirty shit my dad reads.

Mrs. Clay, my seventh grade Home Ec. teacher, had done some modeling and a few commercials in L.A. before getting married and moving to our town. Everyone liked her because she was cool, and pretty, and kind. She'd always made a big deal over me being the only guy in her class, even joked I was only here for the girls—truth was, I was in her class because I'd rather be dead than take fucking Wood Shop, where guys like me got paddled with 2x4s until Mr. Agostini shook his left hand in your face, showing the stumps that used to be an index and middle finger, as a reminder of the cost of horseplay. She was the only teacher to ever come out and defend me when kids called me Chink—it actually made her angry I never fought back. She was the reason I'd joined the wrestling team in seventh grade. She made me do it, told me I needed to get out of my comfort zone.

At the beginning of sophomore year, it had come out that she'd posed nude in a few girlie mags when she was in college, and a good chunk of the town turned against her. Pastor Mike and his wife led the charge—reminding people of all the young girls in her Home Ec. class, how she was the worst possible role model they could have. I used to see her crying in her car when I walked my sister to school.

After Spring Break, Mrs. Clay announced she was pregnant and would be leaving at the end of the year.

The entire drive back to the city, while Wave and Darcy laughed about what a perv Pastor Mike was, I sat in the back seat and thought about the time I went to say goodbye to Mrs. Clay, how she'd cried at how thoughtful I was and blamed it on the pregnancy, how her husband had smoked on the porch the entire time I was there, how self-conscious I became when Stephanie Dornan showed up halfway through my visit because everything I said had echoed through the empty house and out the screen door.

Remember that time we caught Pastor Mike with the porno mags? I asked.

It's weird, Darcy said, but what I remember was him lecturing us for going to Tower Records. I don't even think about the porno mags.

So I see you kids went to Tower Records. *Duhhh*, Wave said in his best Pastor Mike voice.

Did you guys know, Darcy said in her best Pastor Mike, that rock and roll is a gateway into Satanism. Nonono—*Duhhh*—you can laugh all you want but it's a known fact.

Wave and Darcy laugh, carrying on with their dueling Pastor Mike impersonations, impersonating him in that mocking baritone, punctuating sentences with *Duhhh* because the stuff he was saying was so fucking hilarious as opposed to horrifyingly stupid. Stephanie stumbles through the crowd of metal kids, still crying, and falls into the arms of Heather Campbell, the only girl I'd ever fooled around with—mostly because she was drunk, and I had cigarettes. I think Heather likes me, and I like her too, but it bothers me that we don't even have the same taste in music. I don't know why that matters—maybe it doesn't—but I tell myself it does. Besides, she's practically been with half the school, anyway. Heather wipes Stephanie's tears away, kisses her on the forehead, tells her she's sorry about the records, and Stephanie lays her cheek on Heather's shoulder. Heather looks over at me and shakes her head, and all I can do is shrug.

AC/DC stands for Anti-Christ/Devil Child, Wave says. I can't believe he actually said that. Like any of us listens to fucking AC/DC.

Don't forget W.A.S.P., Darcy says. We Are Satan's People. *Duhhh!*

Why do they do this? I ask. I mean, they're trying way too hard.

Dude, they've been doing this for years, Wave says. When my brother was listening to KISS way back when, my aunt told my mom it stood for Knights In Satan's Service. It was bullshit, but my mom ended up throwing out 8-tracks, puzzles, comics, dolls—all of it. These people are idiots, man. And yes, I include my mom in all of this.

At least your mom's not here, Darcy says.

Well, Wave says, she's here in spirit. Speaking of spirit—

He uncaps the flask and takes another swig of Amaretto. Mr. Dornan storms over, grabs Stephanie by the elbow, tries to pull her out of Heather's arms. One of the metal kids tells him to leave her alone. I don't know his name, but I know the jocks call him Hair Bear because his hair is big and frizzy like that stupid cartoon—and because they're assholes. Mr. Dornan shoves his finger into Hair Bear's chest, probably gave him the same speech on respect he always gave us.

An out-of-towner puts his arm around Mr. Dornan's shoulder and walks him away, and Stephanie tells her father she's never coming home. As they walk past us, the out-of-towner tells Mr. Dornan not to worry, that they're about to put these punks in their place, and then Stephanie tells the out-of-towner to shove it up his wife's ass, and I'm not sure what he's exactly supposed to shove up his wife's ass, but this infuriates the out-of-towner, and Mr. Dornan has to restrain him, apologizing for what she said. The out-of-towner storms off, and Stephanie tells him he'd better walk away, and calls him a dick-sucking faggot, and Heather tries to restrain Stephanie—who drunkenly slumps onto the grass like a child who refuses to be dragged off to bath time.

Jesus Christ, Darcy says. What a bitch.

Stephanie curls up and cries, while Mr. Dornan keeps his wife from running to her, and I look at her on the ground, and then at Darcy, who rolls her eyes because we only see what we want to see.

The night before Mrs. Clay moved, she asked me to be a gentleman and walk Stephanie home. We got to the porch, where she asked Mr. Clay for a cigarette. After asking her whether she was old enough to have one, he finally said he didn't give a damn anymore, that he was quitting anyway, and gave her the whole pack. We walked down the driveway, and she asked me if I wanted one. I asked her if she was afraid people were going to see her, and she asked me if I was afraid of being seen with a girl who's smoking, and I shook my head.

My dad likes you, she said. He says you're a winner. He thinks you can win State by senior year.

Really? What do you think?

Stephanie lit a cigarette, and blew smoke in my face, and I winced and wondered what I'd ever done to deserve that. Now, I'm sure it had more to do with her dad than it did with me but back then, I still feel it was totally uncalled for. We walked past two houses before she stopped again.

You know, she said, what you did to Hiro was messed up.

What did I do to Hiro?

You ditched him. You ditched him for my dad. Do you know how shitty that is?

I didn't ditch him for your dad. I joined the wrestling team. Besides, Mrs. Clay told me I should—

Who cares, dude? You two were like best friends since second grade. You guys were like always on the teeter-totter during recess giggling and shit.

She laughed, and I told her we never rode the teeter-totter, even though we did—all the time. And then I told her I tried to get Hiro to join with me, and she rolled her eyes and blew more smoke in my face.

Yeah, she said. That would've been awesome. Hiro and my dad.

Hey, I said, I tried.

Yeah sure, Wes. You tried really hard.

I turned around, looked back at Mrs. Clay's house. The lights went out and, to this day, I remember how amazingly quiet it got. The neighborhood felt like a ghost town. And Stephanie spat on the ground, and the orange streetlights washed over our skin, and we were the last two people on Earth. I asked her for one of the cigarettes, and she asked me if I'd ever had one. I told her I hadn't, so she asked me what her dad would think of me smoking, and I told her I didn't care what he thought. She smiled and gave me the pack.

You take it, she said. Smoke them all. Do it in front of my dad.

I pulled one out and put it in my mouth, and she told me to put my tongue on the tip of the filter because it would make it last longer. So we stood in the middle of the street and smoked our cigarettes in silence, people glaring at us through their living room windows, and then we went our separate ways.

We hear the rumble of a bulldozer and the crowd cheers. Kurt Loder talks to a reporter from CNN, laughing and shaking his head—the whole thing is a joke. The crowd parts as it makes its way toward the records, tearing up the grass on the courthouse lawn. It pushes the records together, and then backs up, moving to another spot to push them together again, tearing up more grass. Wave takes another swig from the flask, and I realize he's been the only person drinking it, so I ask him for a sip. And that's all I get—a sip.

Jesus Christ, Wave, I say. You drank it all.

Yeah, he says. What're you gonna do, you know?

He smiles, bleary-eyed and bloodshot, and says he's sorry. A group of women stand behind us, holding hands in a circle, heads bowed in prayer.

Did you guys know that Slayer stands for Satan Laughs As You Eternally Rot? Darcy asks.

Really? I say. That's stupid.

Well, Darcy says, it is what it is.

I hated when people said that: it is what it is. What does that even mean? It means we're giving up, that's what that means. Oh well, everything is a huge pile of shit. But hell, it is what it is, right? What about things that aren't what they are? What about things that aren't as they seem? What about the fact that none of these people actually give a shit about the kid lying in a hospital bed with tubes and catheters sticking out of him? What about the fact that most of these assholes are from out of town—that we were going to be the ones left behind to clean up the mess? What about the fact that the ringleader of this legion of morons—this trusted community leader—ran a good person out of town, and all the while he was jerking off to good people just like her?

I guess it is what it is, right?

Pastor Mike's megaphone squeals with feedback, and everyone clamps their hands over their ears. He clears his throat and thanks

Tanuki

THE SUMMER before Henry dropped out of college, his mother died of Histoplasmosis, a fungal infection in the lungs caused by breathing in fecal spores. The neighbors found her lying on the front lawn, perfectly aligned from head to toe, hands clasped over her chest. Henry could only assume the coughing became too much, the fever too ardent, so she got off the couch, stumbled through the mountain of junk she'd accumulated, and headed outside in a desperate bid for fresh air. She probably laid herself on the cool grass, the dew subduing the heat as she faded out.

He could only assume because he wasn't there. He could only tell Tre what he knew—his mother had died from breathing in filth. Tre nodded, his eyes hidden behind black wraparound shades. Henry wondered if the shades ever came off, wondered if Tre was trying to hide the fact that he was famous. Henry knew exactly who Tre was and struggled keeping it to himself.

Tre swiped at his thick, ropy dreadlocks, his hands encased in black latex gloves. They were both wearing those gloves. Henry caught his reflection in Tre's black lenses, pulled the aviators out of his shirt pocket and slid them onto his face.

Aunt Rachel had hired Tre's company to come and haul everything out of the house because it was a rancid mess. Histoplasmosis was commonly transmitted through bat guano, but in the case of Henry's mother, it had come from a family of raccoons living in the crawlspace above her ceiling. Their excrement absorbed into the insulation, swelling like a diaper, sagging the ceiling until the swampy mess burst all over the cluttered dining room table.

Henry's parents had divorced when he was eight. He remembered sitting in the judge's chambers, everyone telling him it would be best if he lived with his father. He remembered his mother kneeling before him, telling him to be a good boy, hugging him a little too hard. He remembered being overpowered by her perfume, looking up at his father, who nodded and told him everything was going to be okay.

The Christmas after the divorce, his father came into his room and told him his mother had wandered into traffic in her underwear, holding a knife, threatening anyone who came near her. This was the last time anyone spoke of his mother, until two weeks ago, when Aunt Rachel called to tell him she'd died. Somewhere in the eleven years since he last saw her, his mother's home had become a maze of milk crates and cardboard boxes, an elephant graveyard of fly-spattered Burger King bags and KFC buckets, her dirty clothes curled on the carpet as if they'd died where they fell. Everything smelled horrible.

I don't understand, Henry had said to Aunt Rachel.

We wanted to help her, Henry, she said. We really did.

Henry peered up at the browned underside of the palm tree in the front yard, its dead fronds like the scales of a fried fish, while Tre scribbled notes on his aluminum clipboard. The Treveon Conroy. Henry could hardly believe it—the same Treveon Conroy who'd played for the Dolphins until a shattered femur against the Redskins. He couldn't wait to tell his father.

You'll never guess who I was with today, Henry would say.

You're kidding. That guy was great.

Remember the Rose Bowl?

Aw, that wasn't his fault. He had a hell of game until that fumble.

Guy was a beast.

He really was. You say anything?

I didn't want to embarrass him.

Hell of a player. Shame what happened.

Henry and his father wouldn't be referring to the broken femur, but the off-season DUI, the overturned Ferrari 360, the dead waitress who rode shotgun, the Vehicular Manslaughter conviction. As he stared at his reflection in Tre's wraparound shades, he remembered the mugshot ESPN had shown over and over, the lingering sadness in Tre's eyes. Henry couldn't stop staring at Tre's massive biceps, the thick veins branching down his forearm like roots—still looked like a pro athlete—and wondered if the sadness was still there, if it had always been there, wondered how Tre ended up working for this hauling company. Henry squinted as he wiped the lenses of his aviators on the hem of his shirt. He put the sunglasses back on and cleared his throat.

So just to warn you, it's a mess in there.

Tre smiled, nodded. Henry's phone buzzed, a text from his aunt wondering if they were inside. Henry gripped the phone tightly. He could hear it creaking in his palm. Seagulls squawked from the roof.

Wouldn't sweat it too much, man, Tre said. I'm sure I've seen worse.

The phone slipped out of Henry's hand as he tried to shove it into his pocket, fell onto the concrete walkway. He picked it up. The front display had cracked. His front teeth scraped across his lower lip as he mouthed the word, Fuck.

Tre placed his giant palm on Henry's temple. Henry took a breath, stifled the urge to recoil. He could smell the latex from Tre's black glove.

It's all right, man, Tre said. I know this is hard.

The marine layer blew a soft breeze up Henry's shirt. He sucked the cool air into his nostrils. They made their way to the front porch, placing disposable painter's masks on their faces. Henry unlocked the door. He looked back, saw his reflection in Tre's shades—aviators, white mask—they looked as though they were about to rob a bank.

Your mother was never the same after Daisy died.

Henry didn't even know he had a sister until the day after his mother's funeral. He was having breakfast in a diner with Aunt Rachel when she told him about Daisy, who'd died in the womb two years before Henry was born. His aunt talked about his mother giving birth to the stillborn child, how she never forgave his father for coercing her into cremating it, how she never got the ashes back.

I don't understand, Henry said. Why didn't anyone tell me?

Aunt Rachel took a breath and looked out the window. Cars slowly made their way up the street, the morning commute, some of them weaving in and out of the lanes, heading toward the freeway exit.

I'm sorry, she said. Your father's an asshole.

Henry lowered his head, and Aunt Rachel placed her cold hand on top of his. She playfully shook his hand and he looked up at her. Her face creased up when she smiled, and Henry realized how long it had been since he'd seen her. He smiled and looked away. She placed a hand on his chin, gently pulled it back to her gaze. Henry went back to his omelet.

After his father had told him about his mother wandering around in her underwear, Henry had imagined she'd died. She'd been hit by a car, bled out, curled into the smashed windshield of a four-door sedan, her last thoughts of him. But maybe his mother thought about Daisy instead. Would her last thoughts have been of the son taken from her, or the corpse she'd carried in her womb for all those months?

Aunt Rachel began to cry. Henry got up, took a seat next to her, put his arm around her while she wiped her tears and blew her nose. She laid her head on his shoulder. His lungs went tight.

The heat and stench hit Henry like a backdraft. The room felt tropical.

Damn, Tre muttered from under the mask.

Boxes were piled in haphazard stacks throughout the living room. Henry stepped over a yellow milk crate filled with empty Coke bottles, the Mexican kind with real cane sugar, and meandered through the wreckage, stopping at the other side of the room. He opened the window. Fresh air swelled through the lace curtains, their swans and tulips billowing higher and higher. He turned back and pointed at the giant, water-damaged hole in the ceiling, the insulation withered and clumped with shit. Tre made his way over, sidestepping a teetering stack of boxes, the bottom box splitting at its seams, colorful sweaters peeking through the fissures. He stopped next to Henry and looked up. Henry glanced at the giant crucifix tattooed on the side of Tre's neck.

That's where the raccoons were, Henry said.

The door to his mother's bedroom was blocked by an old drum kit covered with men's slacks, the spidery pantlegs dangling off the snare and hi-hat. Henry looked over his shoulder at the couch, next to the heap of paper lanterns, stacked and sun-bleached like skulls. The pillow still carried the soft groove from where she laid her head. Henry's old bedroom was blocked off by a mattress. He pointed and told Tre that was where his room was.

You wanna see it? Tre asked.

No, Henry said, it's okay.

Henry turned back to the hole in the ceiling. When he was five, his family had gone on a camping trip in the Angeles National Forest. He and his cousin Alan had happened upon the bloated corpse of a raccoon. Alan poked it with a stick, and Henry couldn't help but notice its hands, shining black as if encased in leather gloves. That an animal could have hands like this, hands that could grab him, made him back away. Alan jammed the stick into the raccoon's mouth, then chased Henry around the woods, trying to poke him with the end of the stick. Henry ran back to the campsite crying to his mother and Aunt Rachel.

After they wiped his tears, he spent the rest of that afternoon playing Old Maid with Aunt Rachel and his mother while Alan hid out in the woods with the pack of Virginia Slims the two of them had stolen together. Henry turned away from the ceiling, wishing his aunt still smoked, still had a pack lying around the house he could steal.

They made their way through the dining room, turning sideways to get through two pillars of boxes filled with VHS tapes. Tre picked up one of the tapes and stared at it, *Ninja vs. Bruce Lee,* a box featuring a nunchuck-wielding man who was clearly not Bruce Lee, a hot pink 99 cent sticker on the bottom right corner. He turned the box over and read the film description. His cheeks made a slight upward turn—even through the mask, Henry could see he was smiling.

I used to watch these flicks with my pops back in the day, Tre said. There was a Bruce L-E, a Bruce L-I, and a Bruce L-E-I. Had a roommate in college, a Film Major. He said these movies were called Brucesploitation.

Really? Henry laughed.

No joke, Tre said. Brucesploitation. All these dudes just trying to make a name off someone else.

They walked past a stack of three clear Rubbermaid containers, all stuffed with baseball mitts—why baseball mitts?—and made their way into the kitchen. Dead flies floated in a thin layer of brown liquid that had settled in the long, rectangular fluorescent light fixture on the ceiling. Nothing turned on when Henry flipped the switch. Tre stared at the rows of ants, trailing along the wall in dotted tributaries, merging in a giant black crush on the stove. Henry stepped to the window over the sink, opened it.

Check this out, he said, gesturing into the back yard.

Tre stepped over the pile of empty cereal boxes, slipping and catching his balance by knocking over the mound of Tupperware on the counter. Earwigs and silverfish scattered from the rubble. He tiptoed through the garbage and made his way to the window. A formation of dressmaker's dummies lined up three by three in the dead, patchy grass.

Damn, Tre said.

Tre shook his head and staggered toward the kitchen island. Henry rested his elbows on the lip of the sink, looked out the window. He pulled down the painter's mask and breathed in the outside air. There was a time when the grass was green, when the swing set was dark blue, not rust-mottled, when there were still swings attached. Next to a weathered doghouse—did they ever have a dog?—sat the rusted husk of their old Weber grill, the bottom rusted open, ashy gray charcoal briquettes spilling onto the grass. An orange tabby climbed into the yard and stood watch on the doghouse roof.

Hey man, Tre said, is this you?

He was pointing at a Polaroid affixed to the refrigerator. Henry tilted his head and narrowed his eyes, but he couldn't see because of the glare.

I don't know. Can I see it?

Tre handed him the Polaroid, reaching over the island. It was him all right. Henry was seven years old, sitting on his bed, hands folded in his lap. Hanging on the wood-paneled wall behind him was the smiling marionette his grandparents brought back from Mexico—red-cheeked and red-nosed, a straw sombrero with a multi-colored band. He'd hated that damned thing. When the light from passing cars hit it just right, it leered at him—dead eyes and handlebar mustache. Every time he took it off the hook and threw it in the closet, his father hung it back and lectured him on putting things away.

Are you scared? his father once asked.

No.

Then why do it? You think your mom likes cleaning up after you?

I'm sorry.

You don't have to be scared of it, if you are.

I'm not.

Good. It's just a toy. Be sure to put your things away from now on.

The marionette was one of the few things he'd left behind, tossed in the back of the closet behind the half-empty box of a Tyco race track that didn't work anymore.

I like those Super Mario bedsheets, man, Tre said.

Henry laughed. He put the picture in his back pocket and looked out the window again. The cat leapt off the roof and prowled the dried and mangy lawn, past the dressmaker dummies, the decomposed bicycle frames—princess castles broken in half, lying flat like turtle shells with all the meat sucked out. The cat settled under a drooping hammock—weighed down with a dilapidated fake Christmas tree, wilted tinsel, chipped glass ball ornaments—coiled itself and closed its eyes.

Was there a box somewhere deep in his mother's closet filled with gifts from Daisy's baby shower—a frilly baby bonnet, a pink blanket— or had those been tossed along with Daisy's ashes? Would Daisy remember the time Tre rushed for 289 yards in the Rose Bowl?

They ever catch those raccoons? Tre asked.

I think so. My aunt says that after my mom died, no one could find them in the house. Then, like a week later, one of them drowned a neighbor's dog.

Drowned a dog?

Yeah, in the pool. Raccoons can do that. They'll latch on around the dog's neck with their little black hands and pull them under. So they called Animal Control and caught them, or at least caught some raccoons.

Henry ran a black latex finger over the sweat collecting in his eyebrow. Tre watched him intently—at least that was Henry's impression. It was hard to know through the painter's mask.

Henry had spent the previous winter fooling around with an Art Major named Marie, who'd dreamed of living in Japan. She talked openly about her ADHD and was obsessed with Anime, which Henry thought was a little strange but overlooked because she had no expectations of who they were. She was just some frantic girl who came into his room when he was alone, and he was just some boy who sat with her and watched *Ghost in the Shell* and *Neon Genesis Evangelion* in silence.

The first time they'd slept together, Marie told him about the raccoons in Japan, how they had no real natural predators because they weren't indigenous, how they ran rampant through the streets and countryside. It had all started from a cartoon called *Rascal the Raccoon,* which was so popular in the 70s that Japanese people starting importing them as pets. Then they realized how aggressive raccoons became when they matured, and let them loose into the wild.

I've always hated raccoons, Henry said. They're fucking awful.

Yeah, Marie said. I guess they could be.

It wasn't until the third time they'd slept together, when Marie finally removed her shirt, that he saw the cute, cartoony raccoon tattooed on her shoulder blade. It wasn't a raccoon, she told him, but a Tanuki, a mythical mischief-maker known for shapeshifting. She'd designed it herself, and he told her he liked it, and she thanked him, and climbed on top of him, and this was the last time they spoke.

I really hate raccoons, Henry said.

I don't blame you, Tre said.

They fought their way through the clutter, the rot, and headed for the front door. He held the door for Tre and looked back at the gaping wound in his mother's ceiling. Clumps of black flies clung to the dangling insulation, fat like tumors.

All These Lives

GIL'S MOTHER calls him in the middle of the news cycle, and he tells her he had no idea Jacob was capable of such a thing, but that was a lie—he's actually been expecting something like this for quite some time now. He'd watched it unfold on the news, men in uniform removing the body bags from Jacob's front door, four in all, prostitutes and street kids who'd gone missing from the County Morgue where Jacob was a coroner. Jacob's father Terry was a mortician by trade. They wouldn't let that go. By the end of the news cycle, he'd learn how these women were found in the basement, embalmed, bandaged from head to toe, seated around a picnic table, sheathed in slinky cocktail dresses of various lengths and colors, wigs placed cockeyed on their scalps. Gil's mother tells him she's buying him a plane ticket, and he needs to come home.

Why wouldn't you come home? his mother says. What's wrong with you? Terry needs us. Lyla—

I'm not coming home, Mom.

We have to be there for Terry. He was Daddy's friend. You don't know what he's going through right now.

The police had found Jacob seated at the head of the table, head lolled back, the top of his skull shattered by the bullet he'd put through the roof of his mouth.

They'd met the summer before Kindergarten. The thought of being in a building full of dead bodies had frightened Gil. He'd asked his mother if they'd see any dead people while they were there. She told him to stop being silly. They walked up the steps, and his father opened the door, and Gil asked once more if they were going to see any dead bodies. His mother took his hand and led him inside.

Terry met them in the lobby. Gil had dreaded meeting this man. When his father said they were going to see the undertaker, he had imagined the professional wrestler, a pale tattooed giant more ghoul than man. But this man looked so kind—a gentle smile, short white hair horseshoeing around his head from one ear to the other. He looked nothing like the Undertaker he'd seen on TV, a monster who'd placed his unconscious opponents into bodybags after decimating them with his finishing move, the Tombstone Piledriver.

Hello young man. My name's Terry. I'm really sorry about your Grandpa. What's your name?

I'm Gilbert Cho.

Well hello, Gilbert Cho. That's a firm grip you got there.

Are you the Undertaker?

Well, Gilbert we actually prefer the term mortician. But yes. I'm one of the good guys. Hey, here comes my son Jacob. You'll like him. You're both the same age.

Jacob came out of the office holding his mother's hand. Gil would never really know Jacob's mother in any profound way. She was a kind, smiling woman who'd slept on the couch while he and Jacob played *Operation*. His memories of her were sparse—she was the reason he'd never lost *Operation*. His fear of waking her, by touching the metal edge with the tweezer, had always made him uneasy. Every time she drifted back into consciousness, she'd tell Gil how well behaved he was, and that was important to him because he knew she was dying—he'd overheard his parents saying so. The other memory was their first meeting, here in the mortuary. His father had noticed her chemotherapy headscarf, and commented on how brave she was. That was the first time he'd seen her beautiful smile.

The last time he'd see that smile would come three years later as she lay in an open casket. Terry would turn to Gil's mother and whisper, This isn't right. It doesn't look like her at all.

Gil and Lyla hug at the Arrivals gate. She's cut her hair back to the bob she wore before high school. She's gained a little weight—and she looks fantastic—she smells of pears. He hadn't seen her in eight years, the summer after graduating college. They were both twenty-two, and at that point, they hadn't spoken in five years. She told him she was headed off to Japan to teach English, following some guy he didn't approve of, and he knew there was nothing to be done.

He grabs his suitcase from Baggage Claim, and they walk to her car, talk a little about their lives. Lyla teaches at the elementary school now, the same one they used to walk home from together—Lyla, Jacob, and Gil—but he already knows all this.

The car pulls onto the off-ramp, and Gil stares out at the sea of brake lights. When they were seventeen, he had told Lyla they couldn't see each other anymore. When she'd asked why, he knew he couldn't tell her. And she told him she wasn't going to wait for him anymore. He watched her walk toward her house, barefoot, her shoulders skipping with each sob. Lyla sighs as the car inches toward the freeway.

Goddamn 880, Lyla says.

It's not so bad, Gil says. You should see the 405.

Oh excuse the fuck outta me, Mr. SoCal. Life is so much grander in Gillywood. I'm sure even the traffic is more intense in Gil A.

Okay, okay, he says. Traffic sucks everywhere. I forgot how much you guys hate us.

Did you just say us? You guys? Jesus man, you've changed.

She laughs and merges onto the freeway. Gil looks over at the car in the next lane, catches the eye of a little girl in a baby seat. She smiles. At his ninth birthday party, Lyla kissed Gil on the lips the way nine-year-olds kiss on the lips, and he told himself he was going to marry her someday. That little girl in the car—he and Lyla could have had one just like her. But things never work out the way the nine-year-olds think they should—the way seventeen- or thirty-year-olds think they should, for that matter—which is why Gil sits next to Lyla with so much to say but nothing to talk about.

As they pass the Oakland Arena—it would always be the Oakland Arena to Gil—he stares at the large red Oracle logo running along its upper rim. He thinks of his father, Joo-won, everyone in town called him Juan—the funeral service, the open casket, how it looked like his father when it had no business looking like his father. It had always bothered Gil when people called him Juan.

Are you thinking about your dad? Lyla asks.

When Gil was fourteen, Joo-won was killed in a car crash in front of the Oakland Arena—Oh, you mean Oracle? people would ask—and by the time they'd pulled him out of the flaming wreckage, he was unrecognizable. Yet looking down at his father, peaceful in his blue pinstriped suit, no one would've known Joo-won had been burned alive. Terry and Joo-won had been good friends since that summer before Kindergarten. He'd made all of the funeral arrangements for free, even though Gil's mother had insisted the insurance would pay for it, and it took years for Gil to forgive Terry for what he'd done to his father. What Gil saw in the casket wasn't his father—it was prosthetics, it was make-up, it was fucking putty—yet no one could help mentioning how much it looked like him, how lifelike he seemed.

Terry, they'd all said, you really did a hell of a number on Juan. I'm so glad I got to see Juan's face one last time, they'd all said. This might not be the time, they'd all said, but what you did with Juan's face was truly artful, Terry.

And this was it. It wasn't his father. It wasn't Joo-won, but Terry's interpretation of Joo-won. It was Juan.

Sorry, Lyla says. None of my business.

Just a little tired, Gil says. Couldn't sleep last night.

Jacob isn't mentioned until the car turns off the freeway and makes its way down the winding, wooded road leading into town. They drive past Terry's mortuary. Lyla's lips tighten.

How's Terry? he asks.

Terrible, she says. Everyone blames him.

Poor guy.

Yeah, she says. And poor Jacob. It's all so sad.

And Gil thinks about what Jacob has done—not only with the bodies of those women, but what he's done to Terry, to Lyla. That day eight years ago, the last time they'd spoken, Lyla talked at great lengths on the many ways in which Gil had broken her heart—how he was the only boy to ever do so—and before he could feel badly for Lyla, she demanded to know why he'd shunned Jacob for all these years, so Gil walked away, told himself he wasn't going to look back. She squinted from the sun, crossed her arms, and told him they were done if he kept walking. He never forgot the hatred he saw on her face as he walked away.

Poor Jacob, my ass, he says.

And he suddenly regrets saying that out loud. Lyla pops a cigarette into her mouth and reaches over to press the lighter. When did she start smoking?

Jacob led Gil into the prep room. It smelled like formaldehyde and cleaning products, the cherry tobacco from Terry's pipe. He slapped the giant metal slab and then leaned against it with the confidence of an expert.

This is where they bring the dead people, Jacob said. They suck all the blood out of the body and replace it with medicine.

Four years later, a pale, flat-chested redhead from the local college would choke on her own vomit. Her overbite, the gapped teeth that mesmerized through slightly parted lips—the first naked woman Gil would ever see. This would also be the moment Jacob chose to tell Gil about the process of embalming—the proper and scientific manner in which glycerin, formalin, and phenol are pumped in through a tube clamped over the carotid while everything else drained out of a tube clamped over the jugular. Jacob's voice would shake as he says all of this—he'd refuse to look at the naked girl on the slab—and none of what Jacob says would matter to Gil. It would always be blood sucked out and replaced with medicine. The sadness he feels when Jacob tells him how Terry will suture her mouth shut will stay with him for the rest of his life.

Jacob jumped off the slab and walked over to a drawer. He pulled out two handfuls of prosthetic eyes and asked Gil if he wanted to play marbles. They sat on the floor and organized the eyes by color. Jacob got the blues and hazels, and Gil got the browns and greens.

After Lyla drops him off at his mother's house, he takes a nap and then drives over to see Terry. He doesn't want to, but his mother insisted he do so. The parking lot is empty.

Terry runs out from behind his desk and gives him a bear hug, tells Gil he's grateful he came, and all Gil wants to do is run away. Terry's eyes are pink and puffy, and sloppy white hair hangs down to his shoulders. Gil remembers how much he hated when the kids in school used to call Terry the Cryptkeeper—the same kids who'd called him Gilly the Gook—but in this moment, he finally sees it.

Terry pulls a bottle of Canadian Mist from his desk drawer and places it on the desk. They drink out of coffee mugs. It tastes like shit.

I can't believe it, Terry says. Gilly Cho—Gilly Cho, in the flesh. Boy I tell you, it's wonderful to see you again after all these years. How long's it been?

Gil looks over Terry's shoulder—the old grandfather clock against the wall ticks and then tocks, and then ticks, and then tocks. He and Jacob used to tap the side of the clock with their shoulders, wobbling the brass pendulum, and laugh as the tiny hammers inside the clock jangled like wind chimes. Why did they find this to be so funny? Terry sips from his mug.

It's been a long time, Gil says.

It's funny, Gilly. There was a time when I'd see you every day. You and Lyla, Jacob—it's a shame, but I understand why you grew apart.

So that's what he told you?

The clock ticks—Gil didn't mean for that to sound as angry as it did—and then it tocks. Grew apart. Is that what Jacob said? Is that what he actually told his father? Gil wonders if he looks as wounded as Terry does—if, in this moment, he looks just as pathetic. Gilly the Gook avoids the Cryptkeeper's gaze, gulps his whiskey, goes for the bottle.

Sorry, Terry, Gil says. It just sounds weird hearing it out loud, I guess.

I completely understand, Terry says. You and Lyla, you've always been close. A lot closer than Jacob and Lyla at any rate. Of course he'd become a third wheel. For what it's worth, Gilly, he never held it against you.

Gil fills the mug. Is that what Jacob told him? He knew god-damn well it had nothing to do with whatever burgeoning romance Gil could've had with Lyla—how could he lie to his father like this? Lying motherfucker. Jacob, you lying motherfucker. He takes a long sip, then refills the mug.

You know, Terry says, Jacob had a girlfriend before this horrible thing. She was a hairdresser. Nice girl.

Gil wants to tell Terry he knows. He'd seen her on the news. Those wigs, the ones placed on the dead women, were stolen from her salon. She'd looked so sad, her two boys standing beside her on the front lawn, hands trembling as she read her apologetic statement, begging the press to respect her privacy. All these lives, Jacob. All these lives. Terry wipes the tears from his cheeks, forces a smile.

But hey, Terry says, your mother sent you to help us forget our troubles, so let's see what we can do about that.

So they drink and laugh, and Gil talks about Los Angeles, and Terry says it's just like old times, and Gil wonders if it ever could be just like old times, and then Terry begins talking about old times. How the boys used to mispronounce Three Musketeers bars as *Three Mus-keeters*. Terry used to call them that—Gil, Jacob, and Lyla—the Three Mus-keeters. They drink to this. How they used to hit the goddamn grandfather clock because it was so funny—yes, of course Terry knew. And they drink to this. How they'd play with their cap guns all through the mortuary—Sheriff Jacob and Gilly the Kid—stand over the open caskets and speak to the dead, solemnly vowing to avenge their deaths. And they drink to this as well. They pour drink after drink, as if they could finally hide from Jacob by crawling into the empty bottle. But he won't stop following them.

You okay, Gilly? Your face, it's really red.

Might be time to cut myself off, Gil says. I'm really sorry, Terry. I wish this hadn't happened to you.

And Terry pours himself one last drink, places the bottle at his feet. He asks him if Jacob had ever told him about embalming his mother, and Gil shakes his head—he had no idea—and prays that's the end of it.

After she died Terry had decided to prep the remains himself. Please stop talking, Gil wants to say. He'd laid her naked on the slab but that in itself was just too much for him, so he locked himself in the office and wept. Did Jacob know he was crying in there? When Jacob came to check on him, jiggled the handle and called out to him, Terry told him he'd be right out, told Jacob to be a good boy and play GameBoy.

Then he finally came out, wanted to apologize to Jacob, hold him, but he couldn't find him anywhere. He found Jacob in the prep room, curled fast asleep around his mother's naked body. Jesus Christ, Jacob. Jesus Christ.

I'd never been so ashamed in my life, Terry says. Not of Jacob, but of myself. How could I do that to him?

They both start to cry, and Gil holds him, tells him it's not his fault. Gil lays his cheek on Terry's shoulder because he can't hold his head up, and Terry feels so light and so frail.

I called my friend Clarence, Terry says, who ran Harmon Family Mortuary at the time, and asked him to come prepare Sharon's body. Jacob and I went to the movies, some Arnold Schwartzeneggar film. We never talked about what he'd done. What could I say?

A few days before Sharon's funeral, Gil remembers the three of them went to see *The Last Action Hero* downtown and then went out for chili dogs. Was that the day? Was he fucking there? His chest tightens up. He can't breathe.

Are you okay, Gilly?

Terry, he says, that Schwartzeneggar movie, was I—

And that's as far as it goes. Gil falls to his knees, crawls over to the wastepaper basket and throws up. Terry comes over and rubs his back, says something—maybe it's about how Gil was there that day—but he can't hear him over the puking.

The first time they'd rattled the grandfather clock, Jacob had asked Gil if he'd wanted to stop time. Then he bumped the side of the clock with his shoulder, and they watched as the pendulum wobbled and finally slowed to a stop.

See? Jacob said. Time stopped. Now we can do whatever we want.

Gil would finally remember this on the flight back home.

Gil wakes up on the couch. There's a key on the desk and a note from Terry saying he had to go take care of something, asks Gil to lock up when he leaves. It's dark outside, and Gil isn't ready to go home yet. He walks over to the drinking fountain, which is right next to the staging room, the last place he'd ever spoken to Jacob, where everything had gone so wrong. He bends into the fountain, takes a very long drink, lets the cold water dribble down his chin.

The last time Gil had left this building, he'd run all the way home. He'd puked out most of the whiskey, but each breath still tightened his guts with dry heaves. He finally made it home and fell face first in the front yard. The cool grass felt good against his face.

Gil, are you okay?

He turned onto his back. Lyla stood over him, dressed only in her nightgown and a ratty cardigan. She was beautiful, the way her face and neck were framed by stars and sky. Gil began crying. She knelt down, cradled his head in her lap. She wasn't wearing any shoes.

What are you doing here? he asked.

Her cold hand went down the collar of his shirt, and goosebumps blistered along his shoulders. He looked into her eyes. She smiled. It was everything he'd so badly wanted, but Jacob had tainted it.

She slid out from under him, holding his head so it wouldn't thump on the lawn, climbed on top of him, moved in to kiss him, grabbed his hands and put them on her breasts.

Wait, he said. We can't do this.

You're right. Let's go to your room.

He grabbed her wrists, placed her arms at her waist. She climbed off of him and backed away.

What's wrong? she asked.

We can't do this. I can't ever do this. I'm sorry.

She looked up at the sky, cleared her throat, turned away. She was crying and he wanted to kill Jacob, but more than that, he wanted to die right there in the grass, wanted to close his eyes and never wake up.

He wipes his mouth and looks inside the moonlit staging room. He's ready to go home.

Gil pulls into his driveway, cuts the engine. Lyla is sitting on the porch, waiting for him. He takes a seat next to her. She pulls a cigarette from her pocket and lights it. The crickets are chirping like crazy.

So when did you start smoking?

She shrugs, blows a stream of smoke. Her lips form a perfect little circle when she does this.

It's been a while, she says.

He nods, and her head tilts upward, and the moon disappears behind a stream of clouds. She takes another drag and gently blows the smoke into his face. He groans, actually groans, and she laughs and shoves his shoulder. A moth flutters around the porch light.

I wasn't trying to hurt you, Gil says. I swear.

Fuck, man, she says. You want to do this now?

And Gil is hit with the urge to tell her everything. He fights it, closes his eyes. Crickets throb around them, the frantic rattle of the moth's wings.

That night you came over, he'd say, Jacob and I got drunk at the mortuary. He said he wanted to show me something. But before he showed me anything, we sat in Terry's office and chased Canadian whiskey with a two-liter of Coke, flipping through old girlie mags Jacob had stashed in his trunk. I kept asking him what he wanted to show me, and he kept telling me to wait, to drink up.

He'd then tell Lyla how after they were drunk, Jacob took him to the staging room. You know, he'd say, where they placed the remains into the open caskets. He'd tell her how Jacob smiled next to the open casket, how his legs seemed wobbly. He'd tell her how he walked over to the casket and looked down to see the old lady. She was thin, dressed in a frilly white shirt and black skirt, lips upturned in a slight smile. Jacob reached into the coffin and unzipped the side of her skirt, laughing as Gil begged him not to do it.

It wasn't funny anymore, he'd tell her. I don't know if it ever was, he'd say.

He'd tell Lyla about how Jacob unzipped her skirt and pulled down her panty hose, how Gil saw her purple panties. She was wearing a thong—not the type of panties you'd see on an old lady. He'd tell her how Jacob pulled at the strap running along her hip and let it snap back, how between fits of laughter, he'd tell Gil everything.

They were your panties, Lyla, he'd say. He'd been stealing your underwear for months, the sick fuck, sneaking them out of the hamper every time we came over to study. There were at least twelve women buried in the cemetery, all wearing your panties.

And Gil would tell Lyla how Jacob couldn't understand why he wasn't amused, why he was upset, why he was shouting. He would tell her how he walked out and kept walking.

He drove alongside me as I walked back into town, he'd tell Lyla, kept asking me to get in the car. I told him to leave me alone, and he kept saying it was just a joke. Then I took off running, turned off the road into the woods where I puked. I was completely freaked out. Jacob parked the car and called for me by the side of the road. I didn't come out until I heard him drive off. And then, he'd say, you found me lying in the grass and, well, you know the rest.

But Gil doesn't say any of this. He sits on his mom's porch, staring up at the stars, and the moth pings desperately against the porch light, and Lyla takes another drag.

Jesus Christ, she says, I'm thirty years old. Why am I still holding onto this?

And Gil pictures Lyla in her white nightgown and cardigan, how she'd walked barefoot in the grass, how she'd stopped on the sidewalk and turned back to him, how she'd shoved her hands into her pockets and made her way back home. All these goddamn lives.

It's just hard to forgive, Gil says.

She leans her head on Gil's shoulder, and he presses his cheek against her scalp. He kisses the top of her head—everything smells like cigarettes—and he concentrates on the moth, tapping against the tempered glass like a drunk who lost his keys.

No, she says. It's really not.

Stay Put

S HE STARED at the Converse One Star box sitting on her coffee table. The box contained dead birds, two, tightly packed. The smaller bird's head was nestled under its companion's beak. She lit a cigarette, no way was she going out on the balcony. Not with him right next door. A shaky smoke trail shivered from her lungs, jittery upward-spinning arabesques.

Boyd had made a habit of leaving inappropriate presents at her doorstep—Norwegian black metal CDs, Korean horror DVDs, glossy sheets of Boris Vallejo-style sword-and-sorcery cheesecake paintings. They were always placed on the center of her door mat, contents completely exposed, with a Post-It marked "Rachel." She'd come home from work and rush them into her apartment with a furtive snatch, muttering soft curses under her breath; she knew he was listening through the thin common wall.

There was no one to turn to when it came to Boyd. None of her neighbors spoke English and they made her uncomfortable with their house shoes, their bleached-out hair, their Raiders jerseys. Rachel looked down at them—breast feathers jutting jagged pinecone shingles—and huffed a gentle flutter of smoke into the box, dusting the birds in a drifting fog. She wondered why she never rejected his offerings.

A Death Metal salvo erupted from Boyd's apartment. Vibrations shimmered through the walls and across her bookcase until a brass candlestick stutter-stepped across the top shelf and toppled to the carpet. She walked over and picked it up, her fingers clenched around the stem. Her nails dug into her palms as she imagined him on the other side engaged in a victory celebration—doubled over, his shiny mollusk face crumpled in a sneer, head snapping back and forth to the thick scraping crunch of an electric guitar. She smashed the candlestick's flared base against the wall in a stabbing motion, the impact shooting rage like quicksilver up her arms. The music stopped, replaced by heavy thuds against the wall. Chipping slivers of drywall flaked onto her carpet.

What the Hell is your problem? she screeched. What makes you think I'd want dead birds? What makes you think anyone would want dead fucking birds?

Rachel stepped back, hurled the candlestick against the wall. Her hands were shaking.

Why can't you take a fucking hint? I don't want your stupid mix CDs or your retarded slasher films! I don't want your Japanese school-girl pornos, you sick freak! Just leave me the fuck alone, you—

The sound of a gunshot cracked through the apartment. Rachel crumpled to the carpet, startled. She'd never heard a real gunshot before, even in her neighborhood, but the sound was unmistakable. A baby cried, breaching the delicate silence. Bile gathered in the back of her throat. Rachel gagged it back.

Ahh Fuck! Boyd shouted. Somebody help me!

Boyd! Boyd, what happened?

I shot myself in the leg and it's bleeding all over!

What? You fucking idiot! How the--? OK, keep calm. Crawl over to the wall, Boyd, I'm going to call 911, OK?

She called 911. They said they were sending someone right away. They told her to sit tight, to keep talking to him. She said she would and hung up.

The ambulance is on its way, Boyd. They need you to stay calm.

Please, Rachel, I'm really scared. Please come over.

The wet pepper musk of the still-burning cigarette drifted into Rachel's nostrils. She looked over to see it on the coffee table, a wilted column of smoking gray ash burning the surface of her table. Rachel sighed and turned back to the wall.

Boyd, I'm right here with you, OK? You gotta keep calm.

It fucking burns!

Boyd, you need to calm the fuck down! The ambulance is on its way, so keep cool, all right?

I'm bleeding everywhere. Please, Rachel, please come over and stay with me.

I'm right here, Boyd, right here on the other side of the wall. Help's on its way. Do you hear me, Boyd? Boyd?

There was no answer. She was afraid he might be dead, but wasn't about to get up and check. For all she knew, this was an elaborate ruse. A muted groan leaked through the wall—she could hear him sniveling. The operator told her to stay put, said it was important that she do so. Rachel began to cry.

Boyd, why the fuck did you give me dead birds? How is that even OK?

They're spooning, he moaned.

What?

They're spooning.

Boyd, I can't understand you. What did you say?

Spooning. Spooning . . .

What? You're slurring your words together. What the fuck are you saying, Boyd? I need to know.

That was how they lay until the paramedics arrived: Rachel curled in a ball, sobbing with her nose pressed against the drywall, and Boyd, buckled and bleeding, his back pressed against a power outlet. A dark speck of blood, no bigger than a nickel, seeped through the floorboards and into her carpet. She could hear the whimpering on the other side.

There's No Connection Here

ONE MORNING during Desert Storm, my buddy Dave Brightman's convoy was driving across the desert when he saw a stray camel walking with its baby. When Dave told us this story, you could tell he was really taken by the sight—in this horrible fucking war, with all the death and killing, a mother camel and her baby just walking across the sand without a care in the world. He turned to the driver, some redneck named O'Brien, and asked him if he could believe it—two guys from hick towns on opposite sides of the United States, watching a camel walk across the desert at sunrise. O'Brien agreed it was a hell of a thing to see, and then he slammed the brakes as a loud explosion obliterated the mother camel and sent the baby spinning through the air.

I don't know a lot about what happened to Dave during his army days, and I don't even know if it's relevant right now, but that camel stepping on the landmine is maybe the only consequential thing he's ever told me about his time in uniform, that baby camel being bent in half as it landed and died on the sand.

I want to tell the sheriff's deputy, a high-strung little guy named Inoue, this story maybe as a way to help him understand what Dave was going through, but every time I try to talk to him he shouts for me to step back and calm down, and when I tell him I am calm, that he's the one shouting, I swear he wants to pistol-whip me, so I take a seat next to Darcy at the patio table and I hold her hand, and she squeezes my hand, so I squeeze back, tell her everything's going to be fine, even though I'm pretty sure Dave is going to die at the hands of stupid cops like Inoue and the back-up he's been screaming for.

Darcy thinks the war changed Dave, and she might be right, but it doesn't explain everything. He'd always been a little off, even back in high school, back when we used to call him Wave, this lanky stoner who'd fasten safety pins through his forearm and laughingly read accounts of GG Allin concerts, only pausing to ask us if we could believe it. And we'd tell him we couldn't, even though we could because it seemed every GG Allin concert was the same dumb shit over and over again. Wave has always been a bit of a wild man, the kind of unpredictable weirdo even the jocks didn't fuck with because nothing good ever came from interactions with Wave. To be completely honest, the only reason I hung out with him was because I'd become an outcast myself once I'd quit the wrestling team.

I had no idea Wave and Darcy were even fucking, until the July after senior year when they told me they were getting married. They made no bones about it being a shotgun wedding, Wave having knocked her up sometime around prom night—but I hope it wasn't on prom night. We hadn't gone to prom, choosing instead to get high in my basement while listening to records. No one knows when Falcon, his actual name, was actually conceived, but I know I woke up in the basement and found Wave and Darcy in my bed when I went upstairs, so I don't want to know how they did it either. They got married at City Hall two weeks later, and a few weeks after that I went off to school in San Diego. Wave joined the army two years later and went off to liberate Kuwait. By the time he came back, he was ranting about oil wells contaminated with radiation—which, according to him, his unit had personally set on fire by order of the United Nations—and insisting we call him Dave from now on.

It all seems so long ago, but that's just how our teenage years are—they never seem like just yesterday the way everything else in life seems to. Falcon's ten years old now, and to hear Darcy describe it, it feels like just yesterday he was learning to crawl, and learning to walk, and singing "Shiny Happy People" to his Power Rangers. But when we talk about high school, she always says it makes her feel old in a way that lets me know how far removed from it she feels, and I totally get that.

What's my point here? I have no idea. I just know Dave isn't well, and sometimes, I do fear for Darcy, and Falcon, and little Beulah.

What ever happened to Steve, or Michael, or Sarah, or Ashley? Jesus Christ, there's an entire world of normal names out there.

It's New Year's Day, 2000, and I'm at Dave and Darcy's home in Lawndale, a little over five miles outside LAX and about two and a half hours away from all my troubles in San Diego. Seohyun left me for some dipshit CHP officer, and I spent the Holidays at my parents' home where my mother told me if I'd dated less white girls I'd have known how to relate to a Korean woman. So when Darcy called me two days after Christmas and told me about how much she and Dave needed to see me, I happily got in my car and lead-footed my way down I-5. Everything was going wonderfully. The kids were very happy to see me, Darcy recounted youthful exploits I barely remembered, and Dave and I drank beers at the backyard patio table telling each other the things we remembered were actual good times. Things seemed to be going pretty well for the Brightman clan, other than the goddamn Y2K bunker Dave had dug into the backyard.

What the hell is that? I asked.

Dave took a drag from his cigarette, and walked over to the bunker, motioned for me. I shook my head, told him I wasn't wearing any shoes. He told me to just take my socks off, that it was fine. The grass was wet and cold.

He unlocked the hatch and led me down the stairs. It was amazing, an entire underground lair underneath his backyard. He said he'd stolen the material from work, that he'd probably lose his job once they found out, but it was a small price to pay in order to keep his family safe from the shit that was coming. I asked him what shit he was referring to exactly.

Well, he said, a lot of the computer programs we use to run the world are formatted to recognize the last two digits of a calendar year. So 1999 is 99, and 2000 will be—

Yeah I know that part, man. I'm just more wondering what you think is going to exactly happen.

The rest of what he said doesn't matter. We've already heard all that shit, and nothing he said would happen actually happened. But I listened politely until he finished, and then he lit a joint and popped *Ragin, Full On* into the tape deck, and I silently watched him get high.

We beg Deputy Inoue to let us talk to him, but he keeps pushing us back, screaming into his walkie-talkie for back-up. He calls it a hostage situation, even though we keep telling him it isn't.

The worst part is he looks at me in a way that isn't necessarily judgmental, but more like a skeptically curious sort of way—Dave and Darcy's idiot neighbors, the ones who'd called the cops, the ones whose lit cigarettes are practically dangling over the fence separating their yards, also looked at me like this whenever time I came around. It's a look I'd seen before from people in our town, the kind of half-pitying glance you give when you're uncertain why a certain person is with these or those people. A concerned teacher had once even asked if everything was going okay for me, if I was on drugs. When I told her I wasn't, she asked if I was gay, which the three of us laughed over later that night.

To be completely honest, keeping in touch with the Brightmans became a bit of a chore as we got older. As Falcon and Beulah's godfather, I came up for their birthdays and sat around with all of Dave's construction worker friends, and all of Darcy's Outback Steakhouse friends, but other than that we didn't really spend a lot of time together anymore. When Darcy told her friends I sold advertising spots on radio programs, they smiled their polite smiles. When I told them it was a little more complicated than that and explained the ins and outs of my job, Dave's friends joked that it sure beats working for a living. And once things got serious with Seohyun, those birthday visits became apologetic phone calls, and shipments of *Crash Bandicoot*, and *Metal Gear Solid*, and *Metal Gear Solid 2*, and *American Girl* dolls, and credit union savings accounts in the kids' names. We just weren't as present in each other's lives anymore, and it pains me to say that, as much as it pains me how much I want to tell Inoue these things because it's clear my friendship with Dave and Darcy confuses him.

We try to explain to Inoue that Dave isn't a dangerous guy, that he's drunk, that he'd let the kids out of the bunker if we were given a chance to talk to him. Dave had rushed the kids into the bunker at 11:55PM, even though we'd watched the footage from New Zealand and Australia earlier in the day, how the new millennium had come without incident. Then we watched the fireworks in Tokyo and Seoul, followed by the rest of Asia. Dave and Darcy went to their bedroom and shouted at one another. Then they had loud sex, so I took the kids to Toys R Us, and then McDonalds.

I didn't know what else to do.

Dave was in the back yard smoking when we came back. Darcy was in the kitchen, so I sent the kids to see their dad, show him all their new toys.

You trying to make us look bad? she said.

What do you mean?

How much money did you spend at Toys R Us?

Who cares? It's just money, you know?

Darcy told me to walk with her. We went to the front porch and sat on the steps. She lit up and asked if I wanted one, and I reminded her I'd quit.

We're broke, she said.

Really? I thought Dave was doing well. What I mean is, I'm sorry. Do you need money?

He spent it all on supplies, cleaned out our entire fucking savings, said money was going to be useless anyway when the shit went down.

Look, just let me help you, okay? I'm a single guy, a newly single guy, with no responsibilities. I'm here for you. So please, just—

You can't fix this shit with money, Wes. He's not well. He hasn't been since Kuwait. You just don't see it because—

Because I'm never around. I know. I'm sorry.

I was going to say because he never shows it to you.

And she started to cry, and I held her hand. She squeezed my hand, so I squeezed back, and I told her I'd love one of those cigarettes now.

At around ten to midnight, Dave stumbled to the glass door leading into the back yard and slid it open. He waved me off when I asked him if he was okay, and Darcy told me to let it go. He gagged and retched, and we heard the sound of seven Miller Lites, and the Kilauea Burger from Islands, spatter on the concrete deck. He and Darcy then screamed at one another as she hosed off the deck. Beulah sat on my lap, and I rubbed her head, and she told me she didn't like that, so I apologized and told her I just liked the way it felt, and she said that didn't matter, so I told her how her honesty was really cool, and made her promise not to take shit from anyone—it didn't seem to matter at the time, saying shit in front of her, as her mother was outside calling her father a stupid fucking asshole, while he told her she was being a real fucking bitch right now.

From their upstairs window, the neighbors watched as Darcy and I tried to stop Dave from taking the kids into the bunker. He shoved me, and I didn't want to shove him back because of the kids, and because the neighbors were pressed up against their window like a couple of perverts.

I followed him inside the bunker, and we argued in front of the kids, and I swear I was making some headway when I heard the sirens and rushed out to see Inoue with his gun drawn, shouting for me to get on my fucking knees. Darcy begged him not to shoot.

Inoue shoved my face into the grass and put his knee in between my shoulder blades. He was going to cuff me until Darcy told him I was trying to help.

Dave, I said, don't come up to shut the door. This guy might shoot you.

Inoue told me to shut my mouth, and he pulled me up by my shirt and shoved me toward Darcy, and Inoue then crept tactically toward Dave, his gun trained on the open bunker. The grass had soaked through my shirt, and it clung to me as if it never wanted me to forget what it felt like to be wet and cold.

There's something I've never told Dave about, partly because there was nothing to it, and partly because Darcy said it was better not to say anything. It happened near the end of sophomore year at college. Dave was off in Kuwait, and Darcy had come up to visit me, left Falcon with her mother for the weekend. I had to pull a lot of strings in the house to get Darcy to stay in what we called the Boom-Boom Room, a mattress and box spring to the right of the attic, and I had to stay in there with her to keep up appearances. The guys in the house really liked her because she gave as good as she got, which I think they respected. Nothing happened, but we did share a bed that weekend, and my brothers called in favors for the rest of the year, but I didn't care. I just wanted to party and get drunk with an old friend I never got to see anymore because I was in school and she was busy with the baby. She looked great, now that she'd stopped dyeing her hair and started dressing like a normal person instead of some kind of vampire priestess or whatever.

The Saturday night before she went back to Falcon, we lay in bed talking about how our lives had gone when she told me something Dave (or Wave at that time) had told her about me, that he'd always admired the way I changed my life, how I'd started as a comic book nerd when we were in middle school, and then became a jock in high school, until I found my way to them.

I mean think about it, she said. When we were all sitting in Mr. Dornan's retarded History class, did you ever picture yourself here? You're a total frat boy now. And we don't judge you for that. I mean, you just have a way of changing it up and being at ease everywhere you go.

Thanks for not judging me by the way, I laughed.

No seriously. It's cool. I know you're not like these other guys here. Honestly, some of them are kinda sweet, which is really shocking by the way. But anyway, Wave joined the army because of you, you know? Sure, he needed a job, but he figured if you could change it up all the time, maybe he could do it just this once and be okay.

I told her I didn't think I really changed that much, and she laughed. She said I had changed, and that someday, I wouldn't have time for people like her or Wave, and no matter how hard I argued, she told me it was fine, that Falcon had changed her too, that people move on—it's not like I kept hanging out with the wrestlers after I quit, or kept playing D&D with dorks like Hiro Nishihara after I joined the wrestling team. People just move on is all.

And I told her I'd never move on from her or Dave, that I was always going to be there for them and for Falcon, and she rolled her eyes and laughed, and then we climbed through the attic window and smoked cigarettes on the roof until it began to rain.

I don't know why I'm thinking about this now, and I don't know why I want to march right back into the bunker to confess all this. I don't know why I'm calling it a confession. My brain is just a mess right now, and it's just throwing out shit over and over again to see what sticks, even if it has nothing to do with anything.

When Dave and I had finally calmed down inside that bunker, he told me all he wanted was to keep his kids safe, so I asked him if he meant like that camel in Kuwait. He asked me why the hell I'd bring that up, and I told him I didn't know, that it just popped into my head for some reason, and he told me to never bring that up again. I wasn't there—I had no idea what the hell I was talking about.

I don't know why I brought that up, but as Darcy crushes my hand in hers, I want so badly to tell Inoue about it, that this man had watched a camel step on a landmine. I want Inoue to think about it because you can't hear a story like that without it meaning something to you. It might not mean the same thing to him that it does for me, but it'll still mean something. Maybe it'll remind Inoue of driving in his cruiser after a long shift that was finally coming to an end. It had been a shitty day. I don't know if this is true, but I'd once heard that during a high speed chase, cops will sometimes box a guy in and lead him into another jurisdiction so it wouldn't be their problem anymore. Maybe that happened to Inoue on that night, that he ended up chasing a suspect in a car stolen in Torrance because the useless morons at Torrance PD chased the guy into Lawndale, and made it Inoue's problem instead of theirs.

Maybe Inoue watched in horror as that stolen car hit a dog— maybe he audibly gasped as he watched the car speed-bump over that dog's carcass. Japanese people love dogs, more than most other Asians. Okay, that's actually not true—it's just something I tell potential clients at my job if they're Japanese (*I once read Japanese people are more affectionate toward dogs than other Asian cultures . . . Yes, I am in fact Korean . . . Well, I've never eaten one haha . . . I'll drink to that!*) but maybe Inoue legitimately loves dogs, and spent the entire ride back to the station thinking about that dog, hit by the stolen car that got away from him.

I don't know. I'm just thinking these things because I just want him to try and understand, just try, to maybe feel something for Dave.

But when I make my way over to Inoue, he tells me that if I'm going to try some Asian crap it won't work, so I ask him what the hell that even means.

The race stuff, he says. You're Asian, and I'm Asian, so you think we have some kind of connection. I'm telling you right now that we don't. I'm Japanese, and you're either Chinese or Korean. There's no connection here, so please sit down and wait while my back-up gets here.

Turns out Inoue is a giant dick, just like every other fucking cop.

And just like that, the children slowly walk out of the bunker with their hands up. Dave warns Inoue better not shoot his kids, and Inoue says, *Or what?* and he winces because he clearly regrets saying that. Darcy runs over and grabs her children, ignoring Inoue's orders, telling him he'd better not shoot her kids, and his voice cracks a little when he says he doesn't shoot children. I ask the neighbors if they're enjoying the show, and the little red cherries on their cigarettes wiggle back and forth as they shake their heads.

Darcy tells me to watch the kids as she walks to the bunker and Inoue tells her not to make another move, which she ignores. She descends the steps leading into the bunker, and Inoue finally turns his attention to the neighbors, shouting at them to move back into their homes, which they don't. The hatch slams shut.

Another deputy pops up in the neighbor's back yard, gun trained, shouting at them—*Freeze! On the ground now!*—and they scream and drop to the ground. He looks over at Inoue, asks what the hell he's doing in Dave's yard, and then realizes he's at the wrong place, and Inoue tells me it isn't funny. But it is. It's the only funny thing that's happened the entire night, those nosy assholes screaming and cowering at gunpoint, and I laugh so hard, the kids start laughing with me.

This isn't funny sir, the other deputy shouts. I'm being serious right now. It's not a goddamn joke, asshole.

I tell him to watch his language around the kids, and he tells me to stop laughing, so I tell him to watch his language again, because these guys are a bunch of clowns, and the deputy storms out of the neighbor's yard and into Dave's, where he gets in my face and dares me to laugh again, and I want to tell him I never stopped. Inoue calls him over, and the two begin to talk. We hear the faint sound of propellers in the distance. The tips of the neighbors' cigarettes tip upward, like tiny red dog noses, as they follow the sound of the chopper.

Oh crap, Falcon shouts. The ghetto bird's coming.

I tell him not to call it that, and Beulah says this is all bullshit, and Falcon's mouth slacks open as he watches me not say anything about her saying that.

Inoue calls me over, says I'll need to answer some questions—not now, but after the tactical unit extracts Darcy and Dave, and I ask him why the hell that's necessary at this point, and the other deputy, Fernandez, asks me if Dave has weapons in that bunker, and now I want to tell Fernandez about the exploding camel, but he grabs me by the arm and walks me to the fence, toward the neighbors who still haven't gone into their homes, even though Fernandez shouts for them to move inside. The helicopter gets closer and closer.

The guy in the bunker, Fernandez says, Brightman—did you know he was placed on a 5150 a couple days after Thanksgiving?

Am I supposed to know this? That seems like none of my business.

Fernandez shuts his eyes, and his eyebrows furrow. He snaps his head in the direction of the neighbors and tells them to get their asses inside before things get out of control. He turns to me, cheeks puffed out, knowing they're not going to move.

That your Mercedes out front? he asks.

It's leased.

Yeah, I figured it was yours.

I have to lean in, because the chopper is close, and his breath smells like coffee, and it's amazing how loud helicopters are when they're hovering directly overhead and you can feel their power full-on. I squint as Fernandez is bathed in the whiteness of the spotlight above us.

Let me ask you something, he shouts. What the hell is guy like you doing with people like this? I look at you and I see a guy who's got it all together. These people, this neighborhood, it's just . . . A guy like you, man, what's the deal?

The kids stand with Inoue, who pours a bag of M&Ms into their cupped hands. He leans over and says something to Falcon, who nods. His coat is draped over Beulah's shoulders. I turn back to Fernandez, tell him I don't know, and he nods, even though he can't hear me over the helicopter spotlighting the bunker, and I wonder if Falcon calls it a ghetto bird in front of Inoue, who ushers them toward the side gate.

Falcon looks back at me, and Fernandez tells me not to worry about the kids, that they'll be fine, and it really feels like I'll never see them again, that this is the end of the road for all of us.

This Is Not Happening

A TALL MAN dressed in a Grim Reaper costume walks into first period AP Government with a California Highway Patrol officer. The Grim Reaper points at Casey and tells her to step forward. She gets up and walks over to him, looking back at Harold like he has any say in whether she should stay or go. The CHP officer steps forward. He reminds Harold of a hawk—keenly hooked nose, sharp eyes. The class begins whispering, their murmurs seeping into the back of Harold's skull like voices recorded through a cheap microphone.

Every 15 minutes, the officer says, someone in the United States is killed or injured in an alcohol-related incident.

Harold unwraps a piece of gum, shoves it into his mouth, then another.

Every spring, the school runs a program called Every 15 Minutes to underscore the dangers of drunk driving. The Grim Reaper appears, removes random students from class every 15 minutes, paints their faces ghoulish white. Then they return to class—the Walking Dead— silent reminders of what's at stake when people drive drunk. Harold looks down at his desk, blinks, prays this is all some hallucination from the joint he and Alfonso shared in the 7-Eleven parking lot. His eyelids stutter shut, then stutter open. The Grim Reaper puts his hand on Casey's shoulder. Officer Hawk-face clears his throat, narrows his eyes.

Casey is now another statistic, he says.

Casey looks at Harold—everyone does. He slouches back in his chair and looks up at the ceiling, thinks about the bag of Doritos in his locker. The officer reads her mock obituary, which Harold tunes out.

He constructs his own—a little more honest, a little more pertinent to Casey's life story:

Casey Lynn Gadsen, born May 19, was killed on April 12 when her car was struck by a drunk driver. She was Student Council Treasurer and loved photography. On a Model U.N. trip in January, she let Jared Chang fingerbang her, while her boyfriend left numerous texts because he hadn't heard from her all day and was worried sick. She then texted him at two a.m. saying she was tired, going to bed, would call later. He then left three messages, asking her to call back because he wanted to make sure she was okay. She never called back, didn't own up to what happened on that trip until the night before her "death," when she told her boyfriend how it meant nothing because everyone was really drunk. "Besides," she said, "Jared's with Liz Kovalenko now and he loves her, and I love you," which made her now boyfriend laugh so hard he couldn't breathe straight. His breathing was still fucked up the next morning, so he and his friend Alfonso got high before AP Government, the deep tokes being the only thing keeping him from hyperventilating.

Hawk-face and the Grim Reaper lead her out. Casey looks back at Harold.

Casey is survived by her father, Wallace; her mother, Sharon; her brother, Derek; and Chang's finger.

The door clicks shut. Casey's gone. Some girls start crying like it's all some kind of shock, like they hadn't already gone through the exact same shit last year. Chang looks at him, sadly shakes his head. Harold shrugs.

Harold had spent his night planning on how to break the news to Liz Kovalenko, how her boyfriend fingerbanged his girlfriend back in January, but she's not in class today. She probably would have just blamed him anyway, and Chang would have kicked the shit out of him. He asks Mr. Davis if he can get a drink of water. Mr. Davis tells him to stay put, so Harold shuts his eyes, drifts into the darkness.

Liz is in Drama Club. She's probably going to take part in the car crash they'll stage on the football field after lunch, a cheap replication of true loss. Chang will probably cry when he sees her wrecked body, won't even once think about that Model U.N. trip to Virginia.

Harold opens his eyes, and Mr. Davis tries to get things back on track, but no one can concentrate on the 24th Amendment, or poll taxes, or Jim Crow Laws.

The Walking Dead, and the kids from the staged accident, will be sequestered overnight at the Best Western in Redondo. Their friends and families will think about what it means to lose someone to drunk driving. The next morning, there will be an assembly where everyone can reflect upon their feelings of loss. For one entire night, everyone gets to pretend to lose someone. Harold won't have to pretend—his brother Dana was killed two years ago by a drunk driver. His mother spoke at last year's Every 15 Minutes assembly about what Dana's death did to their family. She'd told them she and her husband had recently divorced because of it, which was bullshit because all they did was fight, even when Dana was alive.

Harold closes his eyes, dreading that assembly, sitting through the video showing what happens to everyone involved in a drunk driving fatality—the victims going to the coroner, the drivers being booked, jailed, charged. The video ends with a montage, pictures of the kids who "died," so their "deaths" can be forever etched in everyone's memories. They're not even real victims, just a bunch of kids playing dress-up. How can he take any of this seriously?

Harold thinks about the man that left his car T-boned against Dana's car at the intersection, how that man fled the scene, how the police caught him a mile from the accident with a .19 BAC. His mother has cried every Fourth of July since the one Dana spent at his girlfriend's house, the one he never made it back from.

Harold opens his eyes. He pops a stick of gum, then another, chomps furiously. He really wants a drink of water.

The bell rings, and everyone gathers their books. Mr. Davis asks him if he's okay.

You shoved an entire pack of gum into your mouth, Mr. Davis says.

My mouth is dry, Harold says.

Mr. Davis shakes his head. Harold closes his textbook, looks down at his notes—doodles of lop-sided cars, deflated faces, jagged spirals. For the next couple days, everyone will act like they care about drunk driving, pledge not to do it. A few years later, one of them will get into a car, swear to their friends that they're okay, head out on the road. And then some other kid will get to hold his mom's hand once a year while they watch the fireworks on TV.

Harold and Alfonso share a joint in his car during lunch. This bullshit song comes on, and Harold skips ahead to the next track—Casey likes that bullshit song. He reclines the driver's seat, watches the thick, sweet smoke roll across the ceiling.

They get out of the car and walk toward the cafeteria, lunches in hand. By the time they notice the young CHP officer at the entrance, it's too late to turn back. The officer says hello, leans in and looks into their half-shut eyes, sniffs the air. The gold name tag on his chest reads Fishman, and Harold concentrates on it because the officer is smiling. The officer looks down at the bag crinkling in Harold's hands, then back up into Harold's eyes.

Don't be stupid, fellas, Officer Fishman says. Not today.

The boys nod, walk into the cafeteria, take a seat at a table. Harold opens his bag, pulls out the sandwich and Coke, remembers the Doritos in his locker. Could anything possibly go right today?

Casey and the other Walking Dead kids eat silently at a table by themselves, skulls painted on their faces. Black eye socket circles painted around their eyes, the black tally marks drawn on their white lips to look like teeth. Someone even took the trouble to shade in their cheekbones.

Casey sees Harold, looks down. Harold doesn't know what to do with his hands. She sits, head lowered, spooning yogurt into her mouth. Harold scans the room for Chang, who's sitting with some other jocks, laughing, pounding the table, making spectacles of themselves. Harold takes a bite of his sandwich, chews on a rubbery piece of lettuce. Mayonnaise is all he tastes.

Holy shit, Alfonso says. Check it out.

He looks out the window of the cafeteria, sees Officer Fishman, arms crossed, laughing with Mrs. Bowen, who was captain of the cheerleading team when she went here. Once when they were drunk, Alfonso told Harold he liked to jerk off to the picture of her in the trophy case, the one where she's seventeen and doing the Chinese Splits in her pleated skirt. Every time Harold sees her, he tries not to laugh at the image of Alfonso standing in front of the trophy case, committing that photo to memory. Alfonso asks if he's staring at her ass. Harold doesn't answer.

Yeah, Alfonso says. I'm staring at that ass too.

Harold examines Officer Fishman—squarejaw, dimpled chin, intense blue eyes—he looks like the kind of guy that comes out of the Jiu Jitsu studio down the street from where his mother works, the kind of guy that wears tight T-shirts and faded jeans, calls everyone Bro. Does Mrs. Bowen's husband know she giggles with other men?

Officer Fishman smiles at her, nods, thumbs locked around his belt loops. He's probably thinking about fingerbanging her.

Dude, Alfonso says, you know who that cop is?

Harold shakes his head.

That's Tad Fishman. That's Mrs. Bowen's brother.

Why would I know that?

The guy holds the state record for assists and field goal percentage.

He can shove his records up his dick-hole.

Whatever, man. Dude's a baller. I bet he got mad pussy when he went here.

A kid drops his tray, the fork and spoon jangling on the tiles, the plastic cup bouncing and spilling his fountain drink everywhere. Ice cubes scatter across the floor like diamonds.

Everyone claps as though this were the first time some idiot dropped his lunch tray, and the kid drops to his knees, desperately putting everything back on the tray as if the celebration will stop once he puts his tray on the rack. The ice is so wet and shiny against the tiles.

Harold's eyes struggle to stay open. He finally forces them open, realizes he's jumping forward in time—it's as if he has a time machine in his head. He closes his eyes. The kid's kneeling in front of his tray looking like a dipshit. He opens them again. The tray is gone, the kid kneeling with napkins, wiping up his mess. The ice cubes are gone, and Harold is sad about it—they looked so cool spread out like that.

I think Liz Kovalenko's gonna be in the crash, Harold says.

Yeah?

She wasn't in AP Government.

You think Chang knows?

The janitor wheels out a mop and bucket. The kid walks away, and everyone claps again. He raises his arms, smiling in triumph, as someone else cleans up his mess. Chang and his crew laugh, give the kid a thumbs-up as he walks past. People start chanting speech, speech, speech, speech. Everyone's so pleased with themselves.

Fuck Chang, Harold says.

Mrs. Bowen hugs her brother and leaves. Fishman sees Harold and winks, presses his thumb and forefinger together, brings them up to his lips. Harold closes his eyes. Everyone disappears.

The crowd parts for Casey. She looks so uncomfortable, all that white paint caked on her face. Harold shoves his Chemistry book into his locker, sees the Homecoming picture taped to the inside of the door. He waits for her to walk past so he can take the picture down—she doesn't walk past. She stands behind him.

The theme was Island Getaway. She's wearing a lei. The backdrop—a red sun exploding across a pink sky. They look so stupid in their oversized straw hats. His eyes clamp shut. All he wants is for time to move forward.

After the dance, he and a group of friends had rented a room at the Best Western in Manhattan Beach—the same Best Western where the Walking Dead will spend their night. They'd spent most of the night trading shots and getting high on the beach. He and Casey stayed behind after everyone left, sitting on the sand, staring up at the moon, sharing a flask of Wild Turkey. They staggered back to the crowded motel room, stepping over the passed-out bodies. The only place they could lie down was the cold bathroom floor. They held each other, kissed in the dark. The ventilation fan was still on. He swore he heard the ocean.

He presses his forehead into the photo. His eyes open. Nothing's in focus. People start to whisper. He's not going to turn around, even though she wants him to.

The bell rings. It sounds broken—he knows it isn't. A teacher tells everyone to move along to the football field.

Harsh bro, someone says. She's not really dead.

Mind your own business.

Whatever, dude.

He turns around and she's gone. He closes his eyes again, just to make sure.

Harold and Casey were in the driveway unloading his father's minivan when the cops pulled up to the house. They'd just gotten back from watching the fireworks at Redondo—Harold, his mother and father, and Casey. Dana was at his girlfriend Mollie's house. The two of them had planned on leaving the next morning for Portugal. A year after Dana's death, Mollie came to the house, told Harold's parents about the abortion she'd had at the end of that summer. The three of them sat at the table, Mollie crying, telling them she was sorry, Harold's father telling her he understood, his mother sitting straight, staring into space. He'd felt horrible for eavesdropping and went up to his room, remembering how Mollie barely made eye contact with anyone at the funeral, how her arms hung limp when his mother hugged her.

Until the cops showed up, it had been the best night of his life— he and Casey holding hands, watching those explosions bloom over the Pacific Ocean. She'd cried during the finale, all those fireworks clustering together, people cheering, children waving their sparklers into the sky. The cops got out of their squad car, walked up to the porch, where they talked to his parents, and then his father wrapped his arms around his mother, who began to wail.

Your brother's been in an accident, his father said. Walk Casey home and then come right back. We'll be back as soon as we can.

But I want to come with you.

Son, his father said. Please. Stay here.

Harold walked Casey home. Her parents were asleep. They went into her TV den and sat on the couch. Casey fell asleep, her head resting against his heart. He sat there for the rest of the night as she snored softly in his chest, the TV on Mute, angry that his father had called him Son, that he didn't want Harold there.

When he was six, his mother's cat Pepper had kittens. He'd loved those kittens and spent every morning on the couch stroking their soft, velvet skulls. A little kitten they'd named Sasha managed to crawl behind a couch cushion. Harold had no idea Sasha was back there when he sat down, settling into the cushion holding her brother Magic—the one they were going to keep. His mother found Sasha smothered behind the cushion while Harold was at school. He swore to his crying mother it was an accident, swore he'd never meant to do it.

His father sat him down for a talk before bedtime. Harold looked up at him, their faces illuminated by the Nite Lite. His mother had cried all through dinner.

Son, his father said, you have to be careful with them. They're just babies.

Is Mommy okay?

She'll be fine, Son.

Harold's father kissed him on the forehead and walked out, closed the door. In that moment, it seemed like his father only called him Son when he was upset with him. The last time he'd been called Son was three weeks prior, when he'd busted out the living room window with a soccer ball, and his father told him how irresponsible it was to play ball in the house. It was like his father had forgotten Harold's name whenever something upset him. They gave the remaining kittens away the next day, including Magic.

I'm sorry Son, but your mother and I think Magic might be better off in another home.

Pepper was spayed a month later.

Casey woke up, looked into his eyes and tried to smile. Harold asked her why they didn't want him in the hospital with them. He couldn't understand it. She got up and straddled him, unbuttoned her shirt.

But your parents—

They won't wake up.

Her parents didn't wake up, and Harold spent the rest of that night gripping Casey's hips, sliding his tongue into her mouth. They took the condom outside, buried it in the trash bin. Casey held him as birds began chattering in the trees.

The wreckage of a head-on collision, a Volkswagen Golf and a Dodge pick-up, sits at the 50 yard line, right on top of the Spartans logo. Harold watches from the back of the bleachers. The roof of the Golf is crushed down, and he can't help wondering how the roof could cave in like that in a head-on collision. Trevor Gibbs, President of the Drama Club, sits shotgun in the Golf, dazed and bloodied. Liz Kovalenko, the driver, lies face down on the hood of the Golf.

If only this were real. If only this had happened while Chang was at the Model U.N. Conference with Casey. If only Liz, suspecting Chang had a thing for Casey, drove Trevor up to the woods, shared a bottle of Vodka with him, chased it with cans of Red Bull. If only Trevor wasn't gay. Then he could've unbuckled his pants, and Liz could've leaned over, and lowered her head into his lap, dreaming of how she would break the news to Chang. Of course, Liz never would've had the chance to tell Chang, dying in a head-on collision that somehow also managed to mangle her roof. Liz is covered in blood, her arm dangling off the hood. How did she manage to get through the windshield with the roof caved in in like that?

The driver of the pick-up is Darshan Ramachandran, a midfielder on the soccer team. He and Harold were teammates once, until Dana died and Harold quit the team. Darshan gets out of the truck, looks at Liz's body. He freaks out, screams Holy Fuck over and over. Harold smiles, blinks, or at least he thinks he blinks. At any rate, his eyes close, then open again. It's possible he's not even smiling right now. He runs his fingers over his lips.

A CHP cruiser pulls up—sirens blaring, red and blue lights flashing. Officer Hawk-face steps out of the cruiser and confronts Darshan, while the other, local basketball hero Tad Fishman, jogs over to check on Trevor. They chase Darshan—who tries to escape on foot, but falls to the grass. Harold tries not to laugh as the officers pull Darshan to his feet. Fishman chuckles as they dust the white chalk off of Darshan's knees and cuff him. Hawk-face shoots Fishman a dirty look. Harold looks down four rows at Chang, who genuinely looks concerned—what a fucking idiot.

An ambulance comes, followed by a white van, an old Dodge Ram with COUNTY CORONER painted on the side, and Harold laughs. A police chopper flies over the crowd. Harold shields his eyes to look up at it, gleaming in the sun, the propellers slicing through the daylight. There was no helicopter to help Dana, but where would it have landed if there were? He turns to Alfonso.

Dude I'm really high right now.

Are you crazy? Alfonso says. Knock it off.

A cool breeze hits Harold's face, and he closes his eyes, just to rest them for a bit. Alfonso nudges him awake, tells him to stop being a dick. Now there's a fire engine on the scene. The Walking Dead kids are sitting in the front row, the breeze sifting through their scalps, their hair fluttering. It's a beautiful day.

Liz is strapped to a yellow plank, the firefighters performing fake CPR on her, their elbows bending every time they pretend to push down on her breastbone. She's wearing a neckbrace, an oxygen mask. Casey's hands cover her mouth, something she does when she's upset. She did this last night, cupped her hands over her mouth, when she kept saying she was sorry over and over again. Harold is thirsty.

They wheel Liz to the ambulance. The freshman girls sitting in front of Harold start to shake and sob. He leans over and tells them she's not really dead, and they look at him, and Alfonso yanks him back into his seat. Chang lowers his head, and his shoulders jump up and down, and Harold can hear Chang's low moans from where he's sitting, and one of the offensive linemen puts a giant hand on Chang's back.

Darshan is now in the back seat of the cruiser. The firefighters pry off Trevor's passenger's side door with the jaws of life. The helicopter lands, the force from the propellers flattening the grass, and Chang's wailing is drowned out by the pulsing throb of propellers. Casey turns, looks over her shoulder, the black paint from her eyesockets streaking the white paint on her cheeks, trailing like fireworks before they burn out and disappear into the ocean. Harold knows those tears aren't for him.

Earlier this morning, before the Grim Reaper, Casey had asked Harold if he'd been crying because his eyes were red. He told her he hadn't. She told him she had. He told her he knew. His eyes close, then open, then close. He keeps them shut. Time refuses to stop. Everything still happens.

Later that night, Harold will drive to the Best Western in Manhattan Beach where the Walking Dead are sequestered. He'll sit inside his car and stare up at the windows on the second floor, cheap lighting filtering through cheap curtains, wondering why he took the time to drive out there, wondering what he hoped to accomplish. Out of the corner of his eye, he'll see Chang walking through the parking lot, shoulders hunched, hands deep in his pockets. Chang will stand in front of Harold's car and stare up at the windows. A pair of curtains on the second floor will open up and Liz will look down. She'll press her palm against the glass and Chang will wave to her. A hand will fall onto her shoulder. She'll back away and the curtains will close. Chang will turn around and see Harold sitting behind the wheel. He'll nod and Harold will nod back. Two weeks later, Liz and Chang finally break up. Harold will think about what he saw in the rearview mirror as he pulled out of the parking lot, how Chang leaned against a palm tree and gazed into Liz's window.

Harold's eyes open, and he wonders if Casey can see that he's crying now.

You Will Not Be Redeemed
by the Likes of Them

ARLA BORSTADT asks if the seat across from you is taken, and you assume it's because she wants to move the chair to another table. There are at least two other tables she could take the chair, both congregated by her old jock and preppie friends. Jocks and preppies, you still see them that way—as if it were still 1996, and they hadn't left their lives as doctors and teachers, medical equipment sales reps and stay-at-home dads, in order to spend a long awkward night pretending no one had changed one bit. But 1996 was twenty years ago, and you're now a grown woman who still sees these doctors and teachers, medical equipment sales reps and stay-at-home dads, as jocks and preppies.

Arla swoops into the seat and smiles, elbows propped on the table. She leans forward, so you can hear her over the doughy twenty-something DJ spinning "Tootsie Roll" in a way that makes you feel he's mocking all of you.

Elaine Chong, Arla says. You look stunning. Jesus Christ, how'd you do it?

You tell her you don't want to talk to her, and she leans back, reaches into her purse for a flask. She offers it to you, and you shake your head, and then Arla leans back and takes a pull. The people at the table in front of you glare—Scott Covey, Marilynn Sobel, Mac Jordan, Eli Warren—and you wonder if anyone has changed at all.

You tell Arla about Gorman's appendix as she takes another sip. Chris Gorman had moved back home after spending ten years teaching English in Japan. He begged you to fly back and go with him, as his husband Yutaka had no interest in high school reunions. You finally gave in, because you missed him, even though you'd sworn you'd never come back, even though you still tell yourself you never missed him. You don't want to admit it, but you were relieved when Gorman's appendix burst during your layover at O'Hare. You finally had your way out of this joke, but he still somehow convinced you to make an appearance—because he always convinced you—to show your face and report back on who'd gone bald and who'd gotten fat. He said it would be good for you, and you think about that as Arla finally convinces you to have a drink with her. Maybe you'll end up with alcohol poisoning. Maybe you'll drive home drunk and wrap the rental around a telephone pole—do they still have telephone poles these days? Maybe you'll do something even more stupid, like hurt Arla Borstadt, and Gorman will rue the day he told you it'll be good for you to come to this fucking place. A group of women dance in a circle the way they did back when they were girls who'd narrowed their eyes whenever they saw you walk by.

So you two finally made up, huh? Arla asks.

You ask what that means, and Arla tells you she'd seen Gorman a few months before he flew out to Japan, that he'd told her the two of you weren't on speaking terms, and you think about senior year, that shouting match in the Denny's two blocks from here. You want to tell Arla it was all her fault, that she was the reason things went sour, and the more you think about it, she's always been the reason things went sour in your life. But instead you tell her everything is fine now, that you and Gorman worked through it. Arla says that's really nice to hear.

It's funny, she says. I always knew Chris was gay, you know?

You ask what that has to do with anything, and she shrugs and says she just always knew he was gay, and you tell her you still don't know what that has to do with you and Gorman patching things up, that it's an awkward segue. Back in junior high choir, you and Arla both had solo parts for "O Holy Night," and you'd sung so beautifully, Arla's own father had approached you to tell you what a lovely little songstress you were. The next day, everyone began calling you Chongstress. Gorman told you Arla had come up with the name, just as she'd come up with Ching Chubbs back in fifth grade, but you already knew it was her. She's always been a bitch to you, and that's all you can think about as she looks into your eyes and smiles in a way you'd never thought her capable.

You're right, Arla says. It doesn't have anything to do with anything. It's just how conversations work sometimes, I guess. You know, you say something, I listen, and then respond, and sometimes it's not always in a predictable way, you know?

You tell her you know how conversations work, and she tells you she's not trying to be a bitch. If you want her to leave, she'll leave. She says she's sorry, that she just saw you sitting by yourself, and, you know, she was by herself too, so she thought she'd say hi and reconnect.

Alex Hurley, Arla's boyfriend freshman and sophomore year, sits at the table to your right. He and Lynn Jorgenson hunch over his phone, laughing as he swipes through pictures of his son. *My, oh my, you've gotten fat*—Alex used to say that to you all the time, and you wonder what it might feel like to walk over to his table and tell him how fat he's gotten.

Denis Packer had thrown a huge party at his house Labor Day weekend, the last weekend of the last summer vacation many of them would ever have. You didn't want to go, but Gorman, as always, convinced you it would be fun. What he'd actually said was he'd have fun, and you might too if you'd gotten the stick out of your ass. So you crashed the party, and no one seemed to care Ching Chubbs and Priss Gorman were at the cool kids party. It was senior year after all, and, at the time, it seemed they'd moved past all the bullying of junior and sophomore year. Of freshman year. Junior high. Sixth grade. Fifth.

They truth was, everyone seemed genuinely amused by your presence: *Holy shit you two are actually here that's so crazy!* (it was crazy), and *All right the freaks are here getting freaky!* (awkward high five), and *Sweet, Chongstress in the house! Drink up my friend!* (you didn't). Besides, you weren't the only losers there. Christian Gibbard and the metalheads had shown up as well. You'd always liked the metalheads. They'd always seemed so easygoing, and Gorman loved the fact they still listened to Megadeth and Iron Maiden in the 90s. He said it was charming in a way. In what way, you never asked.

Most of the people you'd talked to were nice, asking if you could believe it was senior year, grabbing your shoulders and shaking them, screaming how you'd all finally made it. Arla, of course, gave lots of dirty looks, but Gorman said that was just her face. You sat on the patio and watched the girls dancing in a circle to the Notorious B.I.G., bragging about filling condoms with his good dick, when Christian Gibbard came over and took a seat.

Bunch of middle class trash, he said.

You laughed and agreed.

They're fucking mean, hateful bitches, all of them.

Whatever, you know?

No. Not whatever. They're fucking mean—mean, hateful bitches.

Marilynn Sobel overheard from the dance circle and glared, so Christian flipped her the bird. She rolled her eyes and went back to Biggie Smalls and his good dick.

Think about it, he said. Girls like Marilynn over there, girls like Arla Borstadt—did you know she made up the Chongstress name?

Thanks for reminding me, dude.

No, I'm on your side, man. These people fucking suck.

Then why are you here?

I don't know man, I'm really drunk. Listen, I'm gonna go now. But I wanted you to know that you're a good person. Everybody thinks so. Shit, I even overheard the basketball assholes talk about how nice you are.

I'm not that nice.

Sure you are. You're a good person and these people are trash. They're all gonna get theirs someday. Trust me.

It was a nice thought, these girls getting what was coming to them. As a matter of fact, you'd told Christian it would be nice as fuck, and the two of you had laughed so loudly, Andrea Hollenbeck shushed you, falling over, laughing as her friends staggered her to her feet.

Christian patted your shoulder in this weirdly gentle way and stumbled off to find his friends. Marilynn looked over her shoulder and sneered. You'd never forget the way she sneered. Who even fucking sneers at people? Seriously.

Arla convinces you to take a smoke break with her. You tell her you're not supposed to smoke on school grounds, and Arla says you can't be serious. You'd already emptied the flask, and after she lights up, she pulls out another one and shrugs, asks how anyone can expect her to survive this fucking night without a real drink.

So I have to ask, Arla says. You're a chef, but you've also managed to lose a lot weight. I'm sorry I keep harping on that, but I mean it as a compliment. Seriously, you look amazing. So how does someone work around food and manage to look the way you do?

You take a drag and tell her you've come to hate food and that alone keeps you miserable enough to stay thin. Arla laughs.

Isn't it weird for a chef to not enjoy food? Arla asks.

Before you can respond, Christian Gibbard startles you, placing a cold hand on your shoulder. You don't return his hug.

I can't believe you two are here together, he says. Arla and Elaine, what an odd couple.

I'm sorry, Arla smiles. I recognize your face, but it's been twenty years.

Oh, no worries. Christian Gibbard. We had PE together.

Oh that's right! You used to get yelled at for walking the track.

They laugh, and you reach into Arla's purse for the flask. Arla asks him if he'd like a sip, and he says, No thanks I'm in recovery, and Arla says, Good for you, and he says he's turned his life around since high school, that he's a different person, a kinder person, and he makes sure to look into your eyes when he says it.

Look, he says, I need to get back to my moron friends, but I wanted to come over to tell Elaine I've always appreciated how nice she was in high school.

You tell him there's no need.

No, seriously. I really appreciate everything you did for me, and I need you to know that. You may not think it means much, but it does to me. It really means a lot. I was a real piece of trash, and I know that. But you saw something in me worth forgiving, and I want to thank you. From one misfit to another, I want to thank you from the bott—

You tell him to just get the fuck out of here.

Jesus Christ, Elaine.

No, it's fine, Arla. I deserve that. Believe me.

Christian leans in, wraps his arms around you, whispers, *Please*. He lets go.

But thank you Elaine, he says. Thank you so much for everything.

Arla asks what that was all about, and you tell her it doesn't matter—because it doesn't. You drop the cigarette butt, smear the black ash across the concrete with your toe. Then you ask Arla for another, and Arla marvels at how quickly you finished that cigarette, and you tell her it's working in food service—cigarette breaks being few and far between—and Arla laughs and says that makes sense.

Listen, Arla says. I treated you like shit back in the day.

By this time, you've finished the second flask. You shake your head—Arla takes your face, holds it in her cold hands, the cigarette flopping up and down as she speaks.

Elaine, you have to listen. I'm really sorry. All that Chongstress shit was fucking racist and I should've known that. I'm really sorry.

You turn your head, slipping from Arla's grasp. You don't want to do this. You didn't even want to talk to her tonight, didn't want to drink with her, didn't want to chainsmoke with her, didn't want to be here with her.

You tell her it's water under the bridge, and she says that's all well and good when you're the one standing on the bridge, and you have no idea what that means.

I tried to make it up to you all senior year, she says, but you kept brushing me off.

You ask her if she can blame you for that, and Andrea Hollenbeck—you don't know what her married name is—walks to her car, yelling, *Put your brother on the phone,* into her phone, as her husband smirks behind her.

Of course not, Arla says. I don't blame anyone. But did you know they still call me Piss Princess? Still. We're adults, Elaine, and some of them still see me as that—Fucking Piss Princess—and I can't even tell you how that makes me feel.

Arla exhales, and the smoke marbles the fluorescent lighting above, and you wonder if moths can die of secondhand smoke.

You and Gorman left the party around 11:30 or so. It wasn't like you were drinking or hooking up, so it seemed like a good time to leave. He convinced you to take him to Denny's, even though you had to get up early and watch your brother in the morning.

As you were leaving, you saw Christian and his buddies behind the row of cars parked in the driveway, staring into the sky, their backs arched, giggling as they swayed back and forth. You told Gorman to hold on because you wanted to thank Christian for saying those nice things, to tell him not to sweat it, that this year was going to be different for people like you. You might have even given him a hug had you not seen what you'd seen.

It's taken you years to convince yourself what you saw didn't matter. What mattered was being a ten-year-old girl brought up to the front of the class, wiping tears as the teacher told that ten-year-old girl's classmates why it was wrong to make fun of someone's nationality and weight problems—*nationality and weight problems*. What mattered was rehearsing day and night for a stupid Christmas concert, only to have some jealous little girl, whose timing was always off because she couldn't even read music, turn it into an opportunity for cruel jokes. Those were the things that mattered.

Those were the things that mattered.

Those were the things that mattered—not the smell, or the glistening streams splattering loudly against Arla's back as she lay groaning in the grass, or wondering if all boys pissed that loudly.

Those things didn't matter, and if they could only see it all through your eyes, they'd all see that. All they had to do was try, see things the way you'd seen them, and they'd finally see what really mattered:

What mattered was earlier at the party, while you were waiting in line for the bathroom, that same girl who'd made fun of your weight, and your race, and that one shining goddamn moment you had in your entire stupid childhood, fell drunkenly against the wall, spilling her drink on her hand. What mattered was she didn't even make eye contact with you while wiping her wet hand on your shoulder. What mattered was she didn't say a word to you the rest of the wait. What mattered was Rebecca Cloonan came out of the bathroom, and the drunk girl screamed *WOOOOO!* and then Rebecca screamed *WOOOOO!* and they giggled, and jumped up and down, and when they were done, the girl went into the bathroom, and slammed the door. What mattered was Rebecca glared as she walked past you, as if witnessing their girlish moment of glee was some kind of intrusion. What mattered was while they were hopping up and down, not one drop of alcohol was spilled from that red plastic cup.

These were the things that mattered. All anyone had to do was look, just look, at everything that had happened.

But no one could ever see things through your eyes—not Gorman, not your therapists, not the culinary school classmates you'd admitted all this to during a team-building trust exercise. No one will ever see things the way you'd seen them.

It's funny, Arla says, how passing out on the grass and waking up soaked in piss really makes you take stock of your life. Like, how the hell did I get there, you know? What did I do to make people piss on me instead of, you know, helping me inside and letting me sleep it off?

And you tell her she can't think of things that way, that people are just assholes.

I was an asshole too. And I really tried to be a better person after that, but it was hard with everyone calling me Piss Princess all the time. But you never called me that. I mean, sure, you blew me off a bunch of times, but at least you never made fun of me like everyone else did. I used to see you and think, like, Man, I'd really like to make it up to Elaine. I just felt like you deserved it more than anyone else.

The first day of senior year, you'd walked past Arla's car on the way home. She turned and gazed at you through the driver's side window, her puffy eyes mudcaked with mascara. You'd thought about saying something, but then remembered Ching Chubbs and Chongstress, remembered the way Arla laughed and said, *You're so MEAN*, whenever Alex Hurley would tell you how fat you'd gotten. Arla spent the rest of the year eating lunch alone, a row of empty seats separating her from Christian and his buddies.

Arla won't stop talking, even after you say you don't want to hear it. They'd driven her home in Lynn Jorgenson's car. Everyone complained about the smell and the wetness, so they put her in the trunk.

They put me in the trunk, Arla says. These were my friends since first grade and they stuffed me in the fucking trunk like a sack of laundry.

Madonna muffled through the stereo speakers—to this day, the song "Secret" will occasionally give Arla panic attacks. The next thing she remembers is staring at the night sky as her friends carried her to the porch by her wrists and ankles. She remembers the wincing disgust on their faces as they gagged from the smell, remembers shivering from the stink, her shirt clinging to her ribs and shoulders, remembers the puke covering the front of her shirt.

My dad hosed me off in the front yard, she says. I remember he kept shooting jets of water in my face, over and over again. It stung so bad and the water kept going in my nose. The neighbors stared from their windows. I don't think he cared too much. I don't blame him. I never wanted to disappoint him, ever. He left me shivering in the garage for almost an hour.

You'll finish your cigarettes in silence after she finally shuts her goddamn mouth. Arla will offer to split an Uber and you'll tell her you need to be alone for a bit, just to clear your head.

I don't blame you, Arla will say. I laid a lot on you. Sorry about that.

And you'll tell Arla she didn't do anything wrong, and walk her to the parking lot. When the Uber comes, you'll hug like old friends. You'll tell each other to take care of yourselves, and you'll watch the white Chevy Cruze drive away before walking to the bleachers.

A security guard will wake you up and ask if you're okay to drive, and you'll tell him you're fine. He'll walk you to the rental car, won't stop asking if you're sure, and you'll never know how you managed to make it back to Gorman's driveway.

The next morning, you'll sit at Gorman's bedside and ask if you should've told Arla the truth, and Gorman will tell you he doesn't know. And you'll say, *She really was a bitch to us wasn't she?* and Gorman will ask if that even matters anymore, and you'll tell him if it doesn't, then it never did. And Gorman will smile a sad smile, and ask you to fetch him a glass of water, and during the flight home, you'll wonder if that smile was because he was actually sad or because he was just tired.

And you'll eventually stop caring about it. Because that's just how life works, even when it doesn't have to.

I'll Allow It, Maybe Just This Once

BRETT LAMONICA had long feathered hair like Bon Jovi. He was three years older than me and his black denim jacket smelled like baby powder and Lucky Strikes. I used to see him smoking with the other metal kids off school grounds, spitting brown tobacco flakes off his tongue.

He wasn't the first person to call me a Chink and far from the last, but he was definitely the only one who'd made it matter. It might have been the way he smiled, like he wanted me to think he was joking, even though he wasn't. He'd put his arm around me when he said it, pulling me into a headlock, or he'd slap me on the back like it was supposed to be good-natured. But he wasn't fooling anyone—not even himself. I'd once asked him to stop, and then he asked me what I was going to do about it, and that was the last time I asked him to stop.

I used to see him after school, bent over the boys' room sink, making sure all the eyeliner was gone before he went home. He'd clench his eyes shut and scrub pink powdered soap into his eyelids. It looked so painful, the way he'd squint at the mirror, his bangs sticking to his cheeks.

He once came over with his dad so he could apologize for squeezing a ketchup bottle down my shirt. He said he was sorry and then went home, and his dad and my dad smoked on the porch. I don't know what they talked about, but I do remember getting hassled for making another boy's father feel sorry for me. A couple days later, I was enrolled in Taekwondo, where a stocky, middle-aged man yelled at me in Korean and told my dad how sensitive I was. Other than that, nothing much changed. Brett kept hooking his arm around my shoulder, and the little fourth-graders never tired of snickering at my pathetic front kicks.

Brett was the lead singer of Vendetta, a hair metal band he'd formed with these guys who were always telling him to lay off of me. I'd once heard them perform "When the Children Cry" in his garage. It was one of two times I'd ever thought about fighting back, about rising from the bicycle seat and pumping the pedals harder and harder as I barreled toward his bewildered bandmates, about leaping off the bike, crashing into him as my ten-speed crashed into one of the amps. But instead, we locked eyes as he held the mic against his lips and sang about a world healed by tears, and I rode away.

Looking back, Vendetta was a pretty good name for a band.

The only other time I thought about fighting back was when he crimped his hair. The only reason I didn't was because he'd changed it back to normal the next day—at least that's what I told myself. He also had a fat lip, which at the time looked really funny. I remember laughing at how dumb he looked, his eyes bloodshot from the pink soap, the water sliding off his overhanging bottom lip like some kind of drooling idiot.

Sometimes, you realize your hands aren't clean and you tell yourself it makes you sick, but that thing you're feeling isn't anything like sickness. It's something else you can't name, even though not naming it means you're either stupid or cruel. And then you shrug and tell yourself there's nothing else to really say about it, but you know that's a lie.

Brett graduated and I didn't see him again until my senior year, a couple months after he'd been kicked out of the Navy. He asked if my parents were home, and I told him they weren't. Then he told me he was here to fix the sink, and I told him I knew that.

So you're working for your dad now? I asked. He didn't say anything.

We walked into the kitchen so I could show him what needed work. You look different, he said. I told him I'd been working out, and he gave me a weird look because how else do you respond to that? He crawled under the kitchen sink and I went back to the living room to unpause *Road Rash 2*.

He finished up and I gave him the money my mom had left. I stood on the porch and watched him walk to the van.

Remember when you crimped your hair? I said.

He stopped, and chuckled, asked why the hell I'd bring that up, so I told him he looked like a fag. He took a breath and shook his head.

Yeah man, he smiled. My dad said the same thing.

He slammed the door and turned the ignition. Guns N' Roses was in the tape deck. We locked eyes as he backed out of the driveway, and I wanted him to call me a Chink again, just one last time, like maybe he'd be the only person I'd make an exception for.

Dead End

S ANDRA STARED at the photos of the hardwood floors, the double oven, the jasmine bushes separating the yard from the driveway— a 1,200 square foot, two-bedroom/two-bath home in Walnut Creek, six blocks from her old middle school. The rent was listed at $1425, which had to be a typo, but Sandra decided to check anyway. It could have been a fresh start, their first in two years—it would've been insane to not, at the very least, ask about this home being offered $1,500 below market price.

Michael Goodman—at least that's what he called himself—wrote her back almost immediately. He told her it wasn't a mistake, that he and his wife had tried working through a rental agency but couldn't find the right kind of tenants. Because they were Christians, they wanted the home to go to a nice family as quickly as possible, so they decided to lower the asking price against their now-former rental agency's wishes. He then asked Sandra to tell him a little about herself.

She placed her phone on the kitchen counter and stared out the window, the window that blared hot sunlight into her eyes every time she'd rinsed the dishes. She smelled the young couple in the unit next door smoking cigarettes on their stoop, and the thought of moving away filled her with genuine excitement. It was honestly the first spark of happiness she'd felt in quite some time, the first spark she'd had in almost three years. Whenever she'd felt down, Brian used to say they just hadn't found their happy ending yet—but those were happier times, a long-ago moment when happy endings actually seemed possible, and whenever she thought of those times, she'd be reminded of their last night together, two and a half years ago, Brian lying half-conscious in a hospice bed.

You have to promise me, he'd said. Nothing but happy endings from here on out, okay?

Was this the happy ending she'd been searching for? This house with a yard? A dog for her son, also named Michael? A fresh start in a new neighborhood where kids wouldn't remember what Michael was like in elementary school? She heard Michael laughing in the living room and told him it was time to take a shower.

Okay, Mom, but can I finish this video?

How long is it?

Nineteen more minutes.

That's a long time, isn't it?

I know but he has to finish this stage. He's almost at the boss.

She walked to the kitchen table—calling it a dining room table would've been an insult to both the table and dining rooms—and opened her laptop. She decided if this really was fate, then she was going to lay all her cards on the table:

> *Dear Mr. Goodman, my name is Sandra Ramirez-Min. My late husband, Brian, was Korean and I am German and Mexican (although I don't speak either language lol). I'm very excited to hear your home is available at the price it was listed, as my son (who's name is also Michael) and I are looking for a fresh start. I am currently attending nursing school at UC Berkeley and will be graduating at the end of summer. As my mother also lives a couple miles from your home, I could relieve the financial burden of placing my son in afterschool care. One of the main reasons I would like to move into your beautiful home is because we could use a fresh start. We are currently living in the two bedroom apartment I shared with my late husband, so I'm sure you can imagine we have lots of painful memories here (and many good ones!). But the other reason*

is Michael himself. My son is on the autism spectrum and it's been a very difficult year for him. He has been sent to the office numerous times because of the constant bullying at school. I honestly feel that the teachers and the staff have grown tired of his justifiable reactions, rather than being proactive about the bullying itself. So moving schools, and getting him away from the kids who've judged him since kindergarten would really help him spread his wings a bit more, I believe this in my heart.

She finished the letter with a few more details about herself—she's always paid rent on time, she has a wonderful relationship with her landlady, that once she becomes a nurse she'd love to own a home as lovely as his—and hit send. Then she saw she'd used the contraction *who's*, instead of the possessive *whose* and wished Brian were still alive to see it—he'd had this annoying habit of correcting her grammar (he'd been an English professor at the local community college), and then marveling at the fact someone born in America struggled to speak properly, at which point Michael would guffaw and chime in with a *Yeah Mom seriously!*

Holy shit, Michael, she said. It's 10:45. I thought you said nineteen more minutes.

There was a second part to the video, Mom. I had to—

Shower, bed, now.

An hour passed before Michael Goodman responded. He told her he was sorry about her son's school situation, that he and his wife had moved to Arizona to be closer to their daughter, that they wanted to settle her in and stay there for a couple years before moving back, as she was having difficulties adjusting due to Asperger's Syndrome.

Is this what fate looked like? His name was Michael—just like her son, just like her father. Of course, after she'd learn the truth, the shame of just saying his name, of remembering the positive connotations she'd drawn from "Goodman," would stretch her guts like pizza dough. But in this moment, she thought of how this was the first time she'd experienced what Brian used to call a *meant-to-be* moment. She'd often felt guilty when she remembered learning she was pregnant, when Brian proposed and told her it was meant to be, when she'd nodded and agreed, even though it hadn't felt that way for her. Of course, her love for Brian had intensified in their eleven years together, and she'd loved Michael since the first sonogram—but it had never felt like fate. And here she was, reading an email from a total stranger, who was moving to Arizona (*Her father's entire family lived in Arizona!*), whose daughter (*In college! Studying to become a clinical nurse!*) was neurodivergent (*Just like Michael!*), knowing God—whom she didn't necessarily believe in—had sent this man, this house, to her.

Mina Seo walks into an Oakland A's-themed bar and grill in Walnut Creek and sees Sandra, the woman who'd been hassling her online for two years, seated in a booth in the back right corner. Sandra was easy to spot because she'd told Mina to look for someone in blue scrubs. It had always struck Mina as odd, a white woman with the name Sandra Min. Of course, it was because she'd married a Korean—Mina had seen pictures of him, not a bad-looking guy, reminded her of her cousin Vincent—but Mina also knew he'd died about four years ago. Why keep that name, as a white woman? Why create that kind of confusion? Why keep the name if you didn't have to?

Sandra stands up and hugs her, thanks her for finally reaching out. Mina does her best to return the hug, even though she isn't much of a hugger, even though she'd only known this woman from the pleading DMs she'd received online.

Just here on business, Mina says, so I thought I'd, you know.

Well it means a lot to finally see you in person.

Mina takes a seat across from Sandra. Behind Sandra's head is a framed Leroy Neiman print, featuring Tony LaRussa clapping in the dugout. Mina had always hated Leroy Neiman. Tacked onto the wall of her father's barbershop in Albany Park were Neiman prints of Arnold Palmer and Michael Jordan, and this restaurant is plastered with them, reminding her of all of the coarse, black Korean hair she'd swept up as a young girl while listening to Cubs games on the radio.

So how are things going? Mina asks. You know, with the house and all that.

Oh I gave that up a long time ago, Sandra says. Dead end.

I'm sorry it happened. I really am.

You don't have to feel bad for me. It's not your fault.

I know but still. I feel terrible it happened to you.

He suckered us both, Mina. It's not anything you did.

Yeah. I guess.

Two days after their email exchange, after filing the necessary paperwork for a credit check, Michael Goodman called Sandra to let him know he and his wife had decided to give her the house. It took four days to get the rental agreement from him, as he was visiting his in-laws in Chicago.

After Sandra signed and emailed the rental agreement, he asked for a favor: because his wife wanted to have the money right away for peace of mind, he asked her to wire the money to her bank account. As it was a bit out of the ordinary, he was willing to forego the last month's rent, as long as she sent first month and the security deposit. So Sandra borrowed half of the money from Brian's father, and used part of Brian's life insurance money to pay the rest. Michael Goodman thanked her and told her he'd mail the keys first thing in the morning.

That evening, she decided to drive Michael into Walnut Creek to see their new home. They talked the entire ride about how they'd decorate the place, how he'd wanted new *Dragon Ball* posters, that the posters he currently had were for *Dragon Ball GT* and *Dragon Ball Kai*, that he wanted *Dragon Ball Super* and *Super Dragon Ball* posters.

You know I don't understand anything you're saying, right? she said.

Mom, I told you. In *Dragon Ball Super*, Goku's a farmer now because Majin Buu—

Yep, whatever poster you want let's get it. Please stop now.

But he didn't stop. He told her all about the defeat of Majin Buu, and how a purple cat god had defeated Goku in spite of him wielding the power of the Super Sage-Men, or something like that. She wasn't really paying attention, punctuating the painfully rare pauses with *uh-huh*'s and *wow*'s.

She pulled up to the house to see a young man and woman unloading a U-Haul truck. She told Michael to wait in the car and got out. Sandra walked up to the U-Haul to find the young man inside the back of the truck, smiling from the top of the ramp.

Who are you? she asked.

My name's Paul. And you are?

What are you doing here, Paul?

Um, moving in?

At first, she thought they must be squatters. She walked back to the car as Paul asked if she was okay. She peered through her driver's side window at Michael, his face lit blue from his phone, tapped on the glass. He looked up and returned her smile before going back to his videos. She called Michael Goodman and left a voicemail. She ended the call and watched her son laugh at his phone. Before she could call the police, she saw the reflection of a young woman's face on her window.

Hi, the young woman said. Is everything okay?

Are you moving into this house? Sandra asked.

We are. I'm Hailey. You already met my husband Paul.

Did you sign a lease?

We did.

With Michael Goodman?

I'm sorry. Who?

Michael Goodman, the man who owns the house.

Sorry, no. The woman who owns the house is named Rebecca Horwitz. We can call her if you'd like.

Sandra asked for clarification, and Hailey responded. And then she asked a follow-up question, and Hailey answered that as well. And that was all it took for Sandra to wander out of the fog, and immediately step off a cliff. She leaned against her car and did everything she could to keep from crying. Hailey called for Paul and asked him to take Michael inside for a snack. She put her arm around Sandra's shoulder and told her not to cry.

He claimed his name was Captain Morgan Steele, and Mina saw through it right away. Even his profile picture was too good to be true—his finely sculpted cheekbones, his square Superman jaw, those intense blue eyes that squinted when he smiled. She'd always loved a man in uniform, particularly the dress blues he'd worn on the dating profile. Of course, fear of mockery made her keep those thoughts to herself—even now, sitting across from Sandra. Captain Steele's photos had checked off all of her boxes (a shelf full of books in his apartment, the Ryne Sandberg jersey, the Rick Sutcliffe bobblehead, a Blue Brindle Pit Bull with floppy ears). He was exactly the kind of man she could fall for—had he been a real person.

Captain Morgan Steele—what an absolute joke of a name. He couldn't even keep it straight, occasionally referring to himself as *Steel* or *Stele*. He'd even once signed off as Michael instead of Morgan, and on another occasion told her his fellow soldiers were happy to know he'd found someone as special as her—no self-respecting Marine would ever call himself a "soldier." He also changed the subject whenever she'd brought up the Cubs, which was odd for a man with a

Cubs logo—the 1911 logo of the bear holding the bat—tattooed on his left shoulder.

Mina had only played along to see where it would lead. She'd never been catfished before, and the truth was, she found it rather funny—it was almost as if she were the one playing the prank. Besides, the only men who'd shown any interest in her dating profile lately seemed to enjoy telling her how much they loved Asian women, or sent photos of hands gripping their erections, so it wasn't as though she'd really had anything better to do with her time.

She'd even done a reverse image search to see whose identity Captain Steele had stolen for this deception. The face in the photos belonged to a Francis Belcher, born in Elgin, Illinois, currently residing in Concord, California. He'd left the Marine Corps three years before Captain Steele had even made contact. As Mina sits and listens to Sandra talk about the progress her son has been making in school, she can't help but think about the fact Belcher had been born about an hour away from where she'd been born, that he lives fifteen minutes away from this Oakland A's themed bar and grill.

I'm rambling, Sandra says.

No, Mina tells her. Not at all. I'm glad Michael's doing well. I'm really happy for him.

Thank you for saying that.

Last November, Sandra had put out a GoFundMe in order to get Michael a service dog for Christmas. Mina placed an anonymous $3,250 donation because, other than her niece, who did she really have to buy presents for? Besides, half of that was from her bonus anyway. Every once in a while, she'd check in on Sandra's social media accounts to see Michael with his dog, a German Shepherd named Trunks. She'd find herself clicking on thumbnails of the boy cuddling his dog, while she sat at her desk and pretended to work. Mina has no idea why she stalks Sandra online. She sometimes tells herself it's because Sandra won't leave her alone, but it isn't that—as a matter of fact, Sandra hadn't reached out to her in over nine months—it was something else, something she couldn't quite manage to reel in and examine, even if she'd wanted to.

After Sandra calmed down, she tried calling Michael Goodman one last time. The number was no longer in service. She began crying again. Hailey embraced her, told her she was sorry this happened.

Listen, Hailey said. My uncle's a retired SFPD detective. I bet he'd help you out.

Really?

He's getting bored in his old age, so he takes on jobs like this all the time. You'd be surprised at the people he helps. I mean, really surprised.

The server brings their food, and Sandra laughs as she thinks about Bob, Hailey's uncle. She tells Mina how Bob specialized in cases in which people had been defrauded by psychics, how he'd made Sandra feel a lot better by telling her stories of the people he'd helped, people who'd lost hundreds of thousands of dollars burying Rolexes and diamond pendants in the forest in order to ward off evil spirits, Rolexes and pendants these psychics would then wear to their trials.

So this is the guy that tracked me down, huh? Mina asks.

I'm sorry about that. I know how intrusive that was.

No, it's fine. I mean, I deserved to know that I hurt people.

Come on, Mina. It wasn't you that hurt me.

It was my bank account. My hands aren't exactly clean here.

How did he get to you?

Sandra has no idea why she asks. She already knows the answer. Bob had already told her how men like this get to girls like Mina, poor young girls who got caught up in the romance of a man at war. Some man in Nigeria had taken on the identity of a young Marine officer deployed in Afghanistan, fed Mina stories of death, and loneliness, and the hope for a fresh start should he make it home. He then told her he wanted to come and see her, but didn't have access to his bank account in a warzone. All she had to do was accept a wire transfer from his sister in California, which she would then withdraw and send to a Western Union office in Florida—Sandra, of course, was the supposed sister in California—where one of his Marine buddies would wire the money to a classified location. There were supposed to be—at least according to Bob—two more wire transfers, but Sandra had come upon Paul and Hailey moving into the home before Michael Goodman could find ways to string her along and nail her with more fraudulent fees.

Bob had told her the young man whose identity was stolen, Francis Belcher, actually lived in Concord, twenty minutes from her mother's home, the home she'd moved into after this mess. Sandra had often thought of reaching out to him—she'd driven past his townhouse countless times on the way to the mall—until Bob finally made her promise she wouldn't.

Well, you know, Mina says. Meet a guy on a dating site, and he seems different from all the other guys you meet. Then it turns out he's some huckster in Nigeria.

I'm sorry it happened.

Me too. Not for me, but for you anyway. I mean, at least I had a few laughs.

You don't have to feel sorry for me either. You live, you learn, and that's about it.

You're right. Shit happens, I guess.

Sandra smiles, tries to make it as reassuring as she can. Shit does happen: you crash a party and meet a grad student who makes you laugh, and then he knocks you up and convinces you to marry him, and then you end up with a beautiful boy you love until it makes you stupid, and then your husband dies eleven years later. Shit happens, but shit isn't always bad—and it's not always good—it's just shit and you deal with it like everyone else.

Sandra then tells Mina about the night she went into labor. She and Brian had been watching *The Postman Always Rings Twice* on PBS. Then her water broke, and she never got to see how the movie ended. She tells her how a few months later, Brian had given her a copy of *The Postman Always Rings Twice* as an anniversary gift, a first edition hardcover from 1934. Sandra remembers how proud he was, all the finagling he'd had to do to get it at a reasonable price. No matter how hard she'd tried to hide it, Brian couldn't help but see how hurt she was. He'd reminded her it was their paper anniversary, how that night was the beginning of his happy ending, that he'd remembered how sad she was they didn't get to finish the movie. She laughs when she thinks about how bleak it had all ended—the novel, that is, not their marriage—and Mina tightens her lips, stares past Sandra's shoulder.

I'm sorry, Sandra says. I'm rambling again.

No, Mina says, not at all. I swear. I'm just looking at the Leroy Neiman behind you. My dad used to have his paintings in his barber shop. Does Michael have thick hair, or did he inherit your genes?

My dad was Mexican, so there was no chance his hair was ever going to be soft.

The thing is, there was a point to Sandra's story—a message of living and learning, of finding tiny pockets of hope in the face of hopelessness, and knowing every story had a happy ending if you could just learn to stop and look—but the moment had passed, so Sandra told herself it didn't matter anymore, even though she knew things never stopped mattering, which had actually been the entire point of her story.

Oh, Mina says. That's too bad.

Mina gets into her Uber and greets her driver, Andrew, who's a bit too loud and peppy for her tastes. He reminds her of the mom from *Bob's Burgers,* whose name she can't place. She only remembers the family's name is Belcher, which elicits a sad chuckle. What would happen if she just showed up on Frances Belcher's doorstep? What would she even say to him? How could she even begin to explain what she'd been through? For the umpteenth time, she tells herself it's a ridiculous idea.

Andrew stops at a red light. The little arrow on his dashboard clicks as he waits for a woman pushing a stroller across the street. The baby in the stroller points to the car, and the mother smiles in an exaggerated way and says, *Yes, car!* Andrew gasps and says, *Hello, little baby!* The stroller makes it to the sidewalk. Andrew waves *Bye-Bye* and makes a right turn.

Isn't it weird? he says. His mommy sees he notices me in the car, and I notice he notices me, and then she and I basically make the same face. I never thought about it, but are we doing it for him, or for each other?

I read that we always make a big deal about things so babies can learn to appreciate the world, she says. It's like, by pretending to care, we're teaching the baby to care.

Interesting. Do you ever feel like you can only pretend to care about something for so long before you finally start caring for real?

She'd once seen a photo of Michael and Trunks sitting on a hillside. It was a photo she'd found herself thinking about more than she probably ought to. The high grass obscured their lower halves, and the dog leaned his head into the boy's chest. Michael was kissing Trunks on the nose. What Mina remembers most from the photo is an old couple in the background, holding hands and smiling at the sweetness of a child and a dog enjoying a day at the park. She wishes there'd been a way to ask Sandra if she'd noticed the elderly man and woman in the background, why she didn't just crop them out.

I guess I really haven't given it much thought, she says. So, how's your day going so far?

Oh, you know. Just got back from dropping someone off at Oakland International. My partner and I are headed to Disneyland tomorrow. Ever been?

My sister goes every summer. They just got back two weeks ago. My niece brings me Mulan stuff every trip.

Andrew peers at her through the rearview, and Mina regrets bringing it up, regrets giving him a new branch of conversation. In the early days of her courtship with Captain Steele, he'd mentioned how much he loved Disney films—that his favorite was *Mulan*, probably because he'd seen all those Facebook photos of her Disneyland souvenirs.

You look like Mulan, Andrew says. That's so crazy.

That's racist, Andrew.

Oh my God you're hilarious. You know I'm right.

Oh sure, with a ten to fifteen pound margin of error, maybe.

Stop it. You look amazing.

They laugh. She remembers the day Captain Steele messaged her while she spent her lunch break crying in her car. She'd told him about how alone she felt, how no one listened to her ideas or took her seriously, how she heard them snickering about her after the meeting. He replied with a YouTube link, the "Reflection" scene from *Mulan*. He told her he was thinking of her, and how he hoped she could gain strength from the song. It was the sort of thing one might get from an actual boyfriend while crying in a car, and it felt like fate was punishing her, reminding her that playing along in this stupid charade made her a fool. It was her favorite song from the movie, and it did actually make her feel better.

Do u feel better? he texted.

I hope its working, he texted.

I love you Mina, he texted. *You are loved by me.*

She sat in the driver's seat and watched the entire clip, vowing to destroy whoever was toying with her.

Two days later, the Captain told her he wanted to visit, but he couldn't access his bank account. The next day, while she was sitting in a meeting, Mina got a notification from her bank. $3,250 had been transferred into her account, and Mina spent the rest of the night ignoring his texts, wondering what would happen if she'd just kept the money and spent it, maybe send Captain Steele pictures from Disneyland, standing with Mulan in front of the flowers arranged to look like Mickey's face, middle fingers raised.

Not a Fever, Not a Dream

FTER MONTHS of trying, the girls downstairs have finally per-
fected the art of infusing butter with cannabis. They're so excited they bring you and Ryan a loaf of banana bread, and Ryan
makes a crack about the time they'd brought over the spaghetti, how
you and he were spitting tiny green flecks into the sink for three days,
and then Tara threatens to take the banana bread back until you convince her you're just kidding.

The next day, Tara and her roommate Denise are the ones laughing
because you and Ryan had eaten half the loaf while watching *Red Heat*.
By your count, you watched *Red Heat* four times that night, letting the
VHS tape spool all the way through the credits until it rewound itself,
and then someone—you're not sure if it was you or if it was Ryan—hit
play again.

We told you to eat like a corner of it, Denise says. What the hell,
guys?

You tell her you weren't feeling anything until it was too late. And
besides, it was good banana bread. The girls laugh, until they realize
how sick you are. Ryan is catatonic, has been since maybe the second
viewing of *Red Heat* when he told you, *I'm oppressively high right now.*
That's how he put it, oppressively high, and you couldn't help but
agree because that's how it felt—oppressive. You tell the girls it's like
you're dying, that every couple minutes or so you'll just start moaning
like you did last Christmas when you had strep and lay in your bed
sweating as "Christmas Wrapping" played on your clock radio.

As Denise walks Ryan to his bedroom and lays him down, Tara
asks if he's okay. You tell her how you woke up that morning and rolled

over to rouse Ryan, who turned to you and asked, *Have you always been Asian?*

She laughs, and you understand why she laughs, but it isn't funny to you. Maybe it's because you're still oppressively high. Maybe it's because Ryan speaking more Korean than you bothers you more than you'd like to admit. Ryan does really enjoy giving you shit for your lack of Korean-ness, likes to say some random phrase in Korean and then ask you if you know what he said, and when you don't, he shakes his head and laughs. Maybe it's because Ryan sometimes does this in front of his girlfriend Jenny, who rolls her eyes and tells him to knock it off—maybe it's because Jenny's Korean. Ryan never means anything by it—it's just two guys fucking with each other—but it's never funny. Maybe it's all these things coming together—in the way that it's always all these things coming together—that doesn't make it funny, but the main reason it isn't funny to you is because when he looked you in the eyes to ask if you'd always been Asian, it was a face you didn't recognize—it was clear he didn't recognize you either.

After he asked the question, Ryan turned over and curled into a ball. The TV screen was bright blue because no one pressed play after *Red Heat* rewound itself. You turned off the VCR and an excited Bill Bellamy told you the next block of videos coming up after the break: Aerosmith, Madonna, and Toni Braxton—but first, Soundgarden's "Black Hole Sun."

During "Black Hole Sun," you told yourself you were high. But you weren't trying to reassure yourself because you were disturbed by the video. You told yourself you were high because it was the only thing that came to mind.

You're high right now, you'd said. Oppressively high.

Ryan rolled onto his stomach. You asked him if he wa hungry and he moaned.

The night you graduated high school, there was a huge party out in the woods with a bonfire and everything. Everybody got hammered, including you. One of two things you clearly remember from that night is the horn sample from Digable Planets' "Rebirth of Slick (Cool Like Dat)" because Mr. Abrams, the soon-to-be former music teacher, told you the sample is from Art Blakey & the Jazz Messengers. You kind of (sort of) remember him being saddened by your ambivalence to jazz. The next morning, you'll wake up in the back seat of Tricia Solano's Mercury Cougar, and see *ART BLAKEY + Jazz Mssngrs* scrawled on your hand, and remember Mr. Abrams telling you he had to go home and finish packing but make sure you listened to more jazz in college.

It takes two days for the banana bread to work itself out of your system. Tara and Denise feel so bad they bring you food the entire time. Denise's boyfriend Gavin, who works at Godfather's, brings pizza every night and asks if you want to smoke a bowl—the hair of the dog that got you high, he says—and the popcorn ceiling looks and sounds like television static, and you're nauseous as he sparks a joint and plays *Battletoads* with Denise. You close your eyes until you wake up alone in the dark.

Ryan doesn't leave his room the entire time. Every time you went in to check on him, he was cocooned in his blanket, groaning with his nose pressed against the wall. When he finally comes out, he asks if you're still his friend, and you say, Yeah, and he hugs you and says, I'm back, baby. Then he laughs, and you look in his eyes and it's clear he really is back.

He wants McDonalds, so you go to McDonalds, and the two of you even sit in a booth instead of going to the Drive-Thru. It feels good to be out. You Supersize a #1 with a 20 piece box of McNuggets. The old lady behind the counter asks Ryan if he's sure he doesn't want to Supersize his Filet-O-Fish and he tells her he needs to save room for the three apple pies. She laughs and you're sad because she's really old and old ladies like her shouldn't be working anymore. They should be relaxing and doing whatever it is old ladies like her enjoy doing.

Boy, she says, you guys sure are hungry.

And Ryan tells her he hasn't been able to keep food down for three days, and she frowns, gives the two of you large milkshakes on the house. You tell her it isn't necessary but she insists.

My son-in-law owns this place, she says. You boys enjoy your day.

On the drive home, you think about what Ryan had told you in Mc-Donalds, how he'd woken from that night the two of you had eaten the banana bread to see you, but it wasn't you—I mean, it was you, he says, just like a white dude version of you—and you just want him to drop it. You just want to move on.

Oh and Jenny broke up with me, he'd said.

What? When?

I guess the morning after we ate that shit. She says I kept saying you were Asian and that you weren't supposed to be. And then I freaked out so bad she said she didn't want to talk to me anymore. That's not how I remember any of this happening, so as far as I'm concerned we broke up this morning.

What the hell is going on right now, man?

I'm still trying to figure it all out. Did you know that when I woke up and you were white, that Jenny was Mexican?

You then asked about Denise and Tara. Were they Mexican as well? Persian? Huguenots with eyepatches and goatees? He laughed and said they were the same.

Anyway, did I say anything weird these past three days? Like freak out about you being Asian?

Look man, you'd told him, I was so fucked up who knows what crazy thing either of us said?

So you're telling me you ate our banana bread and then Quantum Leaped?

Tara laughs as she asks Ryan this question, and once again, you understand why she laughs, but it isn't funny to you. Ryan swears he woke up in another place, a place that was like this one, just different, the main difference being you were a white guy named Vincent Seo. What kind of white guy is named Vincent Seo? Was his middle name Young-jae as well? Did his grandfather call him *Daeji*? Did his mother also pass away the middle of senior year?

Things were just different, Ryan says. Like for instance, Vincent and I were watching *Red Heat* when I passed out, but when I came to we were watching *T2*. Oh and Stallone played the Terminator.

You mean like in *Last Action Hero?* you ask, and he responds, Exactly like *Last Action Hero*, and everyone laughs. Again, this is all very funny, just not to you.

When I told him this was just like *Last Action Hero*, Vincent, the white one, asked me what the hell I was talking about. White Vincent kept saying I was freaking him out, so I went and hid in my room until I woke up back here.

Denise asks if he remembers anything else, and he explains everything he remembers, including "Rebirth of Slick (Cool Like Dat)" by Digable Planets. The last night he'd spent there, Gavin came in and asked if he'd wanted to eat some pizza and smoke a bowl, but he was too scared to leave the room. He says he could hear you, Denise, and Gavin in the living room listening to that song.

He asks everyone if they remember the trumpet section from the song, and you tell him it's from "Stretching" by Art Blakey and the Jazz Messengers.

Jesus Christ, Know-It-All, Tara says, and everyone laughs, and you get why everyone laughs.

But here's the thing, he says. That trumpet section wasn't there. It was the synthesizer from "Ain't Nuthin' But a G Thang" whenever they got to the chorus. And then you remember that other thing from the night of your high school graduation:

After Mr. Abrams shook your hand and went home, you sat alone by the fire for what seemed like an eternity. It was completely silent, even though you could see everyone laughing, and drinking, and having a good time. You swayed back and forth, wondering if you'd lost your hearing. You told yourself you'd never drink again.

And you never did, which only gave Ryan another thing to give you shit over.

Tricia Solano and Amy Pham took a seat across from you and then all the noise returned, the music returned as Snoop Doggy Dogg said something about clockin' a grip like his name was Dolemite. And you want to tell Ryan about this, how every time you hear "Ain't Nuthin' But a G Thang," that line comes back to you and sometimes you groan as if groaning will make the memory go away. You want to tell them everyone how Tricia had asked if you were feeling okay, how Amy said you looked like shit, how the music cut out again and both girls flickered as silhouettes every time the bonfire popped and crackled, how it felt like winter every time they disappeared, how Tricia and Amy walked you to the Mercury Cougar, how Amy wiped your tears and told you it was going to be okay, that you just needed to sleep it off. How you woke up as the sun began to rise, and you felt like you were in a place you didn't belong, that you'd never been the same since that night, as if something had changed—really changed—inside of you, but you still to this day don't know if anything actually changed.

But instead, you force a weak smile as the girls sing the synth loop from "Ain't Nuthin' But a G Thang" over and over and over again— they'll do it all night. Denise passes you the joint, but you hand it straight to Ryan and lean back on the couch, stare at the ceiling, which hisses like TV static.

Undead

J ASON WAS amazed by how much weight Josh had gained—his ginger goatee a sad reminder of where a chin had once been; but more than anything else, it was the labored breathing that made him uneasy. Pulmonary edema, the doctor had called it—lung water. Josh's lungs rattled every time he inhaled, something Jason remembered from his grandfather's heart attack. He used to sit at the old man's feet with his eyes closed, listening to the wheezing static that seeped into the living room, comforting himself by mouthing the words: pulmonary edema. He would die a little over a year later at the age of 71. Josh was nowhere near 71 and here he was, three months on medical leave, congestion frantically knocking around his chest like the balls in a Fisher Price Popcorn Pusher. Jason closed his eyes and fought the urge to mouth pulmonary edema.

So, what's new? Jason asked.

Josh lowered his veggie burger and wiped his mouth. He dropped the crumpled napkin onto the table and batted it back and forth like a cat. They had grown apart their sophomore year—the year Jason discovered sports, girls, and underage drinking, while Josh continually inked rooftop battles featuring Spider-Man and the Hobgoblin across his textbook covers. Bits of Jason's old life dropped off like chestnuts until the person he'd been was an embarrassment to the person he'd become. Tiny pinpricks of humiliation danced along the back of his neck as he stared at Josh's expansive Snake Plissken T-shirt.

I saw Felicity Folds the other day, said Josh.

Who's that?

Do you really not know?

He knew, but smiled and shrugged for the sake of conversation. The diner was empty except for an elderly couple hunched over their water glasses on the other side of the room, a wall lined with amber Christmas lights. Josh took a drink of water, placing the glass back on the coaster, the shape of his hand superimposed across the condensation like a phantom limb.

Remember Jeanette Mullen from Homeroom? Josh asked. That's what she goes by now. She's a porn star, dude. Can you believe it?

Jason took a sip from his straw, even though his glass was empty. The droplets of watered down cola snapping in the straw reminded him of Josh's shallow breathing. He closed his eyes and listened to the tiny water explosions in Josh's chest.

Anyway, Josh said, she was doing an appearance at Dream Girls. She wasn't giving out lap dances or anything, but I did get a Poloroid with her. She said she kind of recognized me.

Jason stared at the melting ice cubes at the bottom of his glass. They seemed so much clearer than the ones from his freezer. He bit into a French fry and stared out the window, the natural light dusting his skin an anemic blue. The wind swirled outside, churning the snow into billowing sheets of mist. Wonderful Christmas Time piped in through the speakers. Paul McCartney's synthesizer reverberated in his ears and he desperately wished Lizzie was with him. He craned his head, looking to get the waitress's attention.

Jason's head swung toward the sound of Josh coughing. He sat helplessly as the phlegm bubbled in Josh's lungs. The older couple on the other side of the restaurant turned and watched. Jason glared at them until they turned away. The coughing settled into a crackling purr as cars drove past the window, pulping the snow under their tires. Josh slammed his fist on the table, breathless, covering his head in his hands.

I'm not gonna last the year, man, he said.

Is that what they told you?

No, but I can feel it.

Come on, Josh. You don't know that.

Josh rubbed his face in both palms and exhaled. Jason prayed Josh would compose himself, prayed he wouldn't have to comfort him. He swore he could see Josh's heart thumping underneath his shirt. Josh rolled his eyes and smiled.

Yeah you're right, he said. Let's just change the subject.

Sounds like a plan. So . . .

Jason trailed off, glancing out the window. The tumbling snow spattered white his field of vision. "Wonderful Christmas Time" faded out of the speakers. Josh took a bite of his burger, took a sip of water.

Hey man, you still drawing? asked Jason.

I'm actually working on a comic.

Really? That's awesome. What's it about?

Christmas Wrapping began to play out through the restaurant. Jason looked up at the speakers as if someone had called his name. Lizzie had once told him it wasn't officially Christmas until she'd heard that song. He clamped his eyes shut, his face collapsing like a car wrapping itself around a telephone pole.

Hey, Jay. You all right, man?

Jason opened his eyes. His mouth was dry.

Just a little headache. So what's your comic about?

Well, there's this scientist, right? And he lives in this world where everyone lives in domed cities because the Earth is now a zombie wasteland. Anyway, his son gets infected with the zombie plague and the only way to save him is to transfer his consciousness into a robot body. So now he's this robot that leaves the city to fight off the zombies who are trying to breach the dome.

Jason heard the sound of sizzling meat and turned to see the waitress delivering a fajita skillet to the old couple's table, the old man's side. The woman had already been served, some kind of grilled chicken breast with a side of fruit. She tried to feed her husband a skewered cantaloupe. The old man screwed up his face, turned away. Jason followed suit.

So anyway, Josh said, he realizes that he's no more human than the zombies are. At least they're still flesh and bone. So he has this crisis of faith where he wonders if his father loves him as a son or as an invention and if the people of the city only care about him because he's a zombie slayer.

The waitress finally came back with a fresh glass of Coke and refilled Josh's water. They thanked her as she walked away. Jason took a vigorous sip through his straw, the carbonation glittering sharply down his throat.

So, then what happens? Jason asked.

I don't know, said Josh. That's the problem. That's always the problem. I get these ideas and I don't know where to go with them.

Two teenage girls giggled their way into the restaurant. They took off their stocking caps and placed them in their coat pockets. Jason watched them shriek and hang on one another, the tips of their hair clinging wet to their cold, red cheeks.

Here's a thought, said Jason. You said it was a plague, so maybe he searches for a cure to save the zombies.

Why would he do that? They're zombies, dude.

Yeah, but they're sick. It's a plague, right?

But they're already dead.

Are they? I always thought zombies were undead.

Undead is still dead, dude. It just means they don't act like it.

The waitress led the girls into the dining area. The shorter of the two led the other one by the hand because the taller one's glasses had fogged over. They started laughing again. The girls were seated in the booth behind Josh's seat. The taller one removed her glasses. She and Jason locked eyes. He lowered his head.

Oh, said Jason. I guess that makes sense.

The taller girl wiped her lenses and put her glasses back on. She leaned over and whispered to her friend. They began to laugh. Jason snatched a small plexiglass menu holder off the table and inspected the dessert specials.

So my mom says you're getting married, said Josh.

I was. We're not sure anymore. That's why I'm spending Christmas up here. She's back home spending it with her dad and stepmom in Garden Grove.

Garden Grove? Sounds like a shithole.

That's because it is.

They laughed. Josh began to cough again. His shoulders hunched, head snapped forward. Jason walked over to Josh's side of the table and began nervously rubbing his palm against Josh's back. The waitress came over and refilled Josh's glass. Everyone was staring. Josh calmed down enough to take a sip of water. He looked into Jason's eyes, panting. Jason clasped his hand on Josh's shoulder and took a deep breath. The trumpet solo from Christmas Wrapping bled into the silence and Jason narrowed his eyes. He focused his attention outside, the dirty, root beer-colored tire tracks gouged into the snow. The icy sludge left behind from tires and boot prints was one of the main reasons he didn't miss winter. He turned to Josh, who was gazing out at the snow dusted evergreens across the street, the gray sky lingering above like a ghost.

I actually need to get going, said Josh.

Yeah. Me too.

After a bit of gentle debate, Jason was able to convince Josh to give him the check. He paid the bill and walked Josh to his car. They shook hands and Josh drove away. The snow now fell in giant chunks, covering the sludge with a fresh coat of white. Jason remembered the first time he brought Lizzie up for the holidays, the sheer delight in her eyes as white flakes fluttered from the pink sky, the snow melting on her cheeks and forehead as she laughed. There was no way he was driving home in this.

He took his phone out of his pocket and called her, listened as she complained about her step-sister's children. Christmas Wrapping was still stuck in his head and he told her he missed her. She laughed and said it couldn't possibly be that bad. They talked for a few more minutes, mostly about his brother's divorce. They said they loved each other and hung up. He walked back inside the diner and took a seat at the counter. The girls were still whispering, giggling into each other's ears. The older couple was gone. He ordered a cup of coffee and read the paper until the snow died down.

They Belong Here Now

J OYCE WRAPPED her arms around her son at the baggage carousel. It never ceased to amaze her, how much weight he'd lost since moving to Korea. She thought he looked unhealthy, even though he seemed fairly happy to see her. Garrett had once been a muscular soldier in the 2nd Infantry, a solidly chiseled young man who'd liked flexing his biceps for his little nieces. Now, he looked like aluminum wires coiled together, bent into a framework that would form the sculpture of the boy he'd once been.

You even smell different, Joyce smiled.

Must be all that Korean food, Garrett said.

He now called himself Jun-seok, because it was in fact his legal name, but Joyce still couldn't help calling him Garrett. The truth was, she didn't want to call him anything else. Garrett was the name she'd given him and, the Korean government be damned, he was still her son. Even Jun-seok had given up correcting her, much to the chagrin of his wife Joo-hee, who'd once answered to Emily, but that wasn't something anyone liked to mention.

Joyce looked over her shoulder, smiled at Joo-hee, who was holding Jun-sang, Garrett's five-year-old son. The boy didn't want to sit still, squirming, twisting on his mother's lap. Joyce smiled and held out her arms, called for him, and the boy stopped, buried his face in his mother's shoulder.

Don't you think Joo-hee's parents might want to see her? Joyce asked.

Let it go, Mom, Garrett said.

When Joo-hee, née Emily Davidson, renounced her American citizenship and moved to Korea, it had strained her relationship with her adoptive parents. Joyce had met Joo-hee's mother Nancy at the wedding. The father had refused to come. She liked Nancy. The two of them had spent their time sneaking cigarettes in back streets, as it seemed practically illegal to smoke anywhere in Seoul. Nancy had cried on Joyce's shoulder the entire wedding, wailing for her darling Emily.

You know this means they're never coming back, don't you? Nancy had said.

We'll make it work, Joyce said. I promise. Even if it kills me, we'll make it—

Oh come off it, Joyce. They found each other here. Not in San Diego, or Oakland, or Chicago. They belong here now. We're never seeing them again.

Joyce stared at the overturned suitcases lazily gliding along the conveyer belt. She ran her fingers through Garrett's coarse black hair, tried to ignore the wincing. She looked back at Jun-sang and winked. Jung-sang giggled into his mother's chest—he had his mother's smile. Joyce couldn't get the sounds of Nancy's sobs out of her head.

She'd never forgotten her promise to Nancy, or the way Nancy had scoffed at that promise. Garrett was finally home again—that was all that mattered. She knew it was only a matter of time, knew it in her heart of hearts, before her family was whole again.

When they'd sent Garrett off to Basic Training, Joyce's oldest son Curt told her he'd never be the same again—Joyce told him to knock it off, that he'd always be the same, sweet boy he'd always been. Deep down, she knew Curt was right. The country was still at war, after all, and she'd seen what Vietnam had done to her late husband, Rich. She'd cried the entire drive from Sacramento to SFO, remembering the day they'd brought him home from the orphanage outside of Seoul. Rich, who'd complained they were too old to raise a baby, burst into tears as he held Garrett for the first official time as his father. As Garrett smiled one last time from the security checkpoint, Joyce collapsed into Curt's arms and cried once more, remembering Rich's tears, his promises to love Garrett and give him a loving home. Curt kept begging her to look, but she couldn't bear it, unable to shake the thoughts of what might happen to Garrett once he was fully trained and sent into a war zone.

Mom, Curt said, just turn around for Christ's sake.

She felt a hand on the small of her back, and turned around to see Garrett, who'd swam against the tide of anxious travelers to come back and say goodbye one last time. And as Garrett kissed her forehead and told her not to cry, she prayed she'd be wrong, that her son would come back exactly like this, that nothing would change, that he'd beat against the waves and make his way back to her as the boy who still kissed his mother and asked her not to cry over him.

When Garrett finally came back, after two deployments, he still kissed her and asked her not to cry, but there was no tenderness in the gesture. While the Garrett who'd left had asked her not to cry because it pained him to see her in distress, the Garrett who'd come back asked her to stop because it agitated him. It was as if all the death he'd seen had drained him of empathy. She didn't want to think of her son in this way, that he was incapable of feeling anything for others, but she'd seen the rage he'd carried inside of him, the way he'd dismissed the problems of others because they'd never seen the manic face of an enemy combatant through the muzzle flash of a Type 81 assault rifle, or watched a German Shepherd step on a landmine, or choked on the charred remains of schoolchildren. Every day, Joyce prayed the boy who went away would come back to her.

On the night of his twenty-sixth birthday, there was an argument at the seafood restaurant where they used to celebrate Rich's birthdays. They were waiting for their appetizers, and for Curt and his family to fight their way through traffic, when a young man approached their table, said he'd noticed Garrett's dog tags—he'd been nervously fiddling with the chain as if they were mysteries of the rosary—and thanked Garrett for his service. Joyce immediately became nervous, as she'd seen the way Garrett screwed up his face every time a stranger thanked him for serving his country. He'd told her it was because he never knew how to respond, but she knew there was more to it than an inability to accept a compliment. Joyce thanked the young man, prayed he'd go away. Garrett sipped his beer, stared up at the man hovering over their quiet birthday meal.

If you don't get out of my face, Garrett said, I'm gonna drag you outside and break every bone in your body.

Garrett, Joyce snapped. Sir, I'm very sorry, it's been a long day and—

I don't understand, the man smiled. I just wanted you to know it meant something to me, you putting your life on the line.

First of all, Garrett said, don't ever interrupt my mother. Secondly, do you know why you put so much focus on guys like me putting our lives on the line? It's guilt. It's because deep down, you want guys like me to die.

When the man asked why Garrett would say such a thing, Garrett laughed and told him how much easier it would've been for everyone had he died because dying made him a martyr, a working stiff who'd done his job, rather than some sadsack who'd killed for people like that man and everyone in else in this goddamn restaurant. Garrett told the man people like him would never know what it was like to take another's life, how they never wanted to think about all the death he'd seen, all the lives he'd taken, that they thanked him because they were too stupid to do anything meaningful. Everything Garrett had said was frighteningly incoherent. She fought the voice that told her, over and over, this was not her son.

So your gratitude means nothing to me, Garrett said. *Thank you for almost dying over there! Thank you for killing all those people, so I can go about my day!* Cool, man. You're welcome, I guess.

The man showed his palms, as if trying to calm a snarling dog, and backed away. He apologized to Joyce for cutting her off, and to Garrett for interrupting his meal. Garret slammed his fist on the table and rose as the man scurried off. It was as though his fist had shattered a pause button, placing the entire restaurant in stasis. The entire room fell silent, and all eyes were fixed on Joyce and her son.

Who else wants to thank me? Garrett asked. You? How about you, Blondie? What about you, fat man? You want to *thank* me for my *putting my life on the line?* You fucking assholes.

Every time Joyce reached up, Garrett swatted her away. Curt ran to the table, grabbed his brother and dragged him away as he cursed everyone in the room, mocked their gratitude, their clean hands.

Joyce had spent the past three years learning Korean. She hadn't been as studious as she could have been, and she'd often joked she had the vocabulary of a five-year-old. Of course, every conversation with Jun-sang was a cruel reminder she couldn't even do that. There were times when Garrett would call her, usually on Christmas and birthdays, and she'd wallow in shame, knowing she couldn't understand the smiling stories her grandson told her. There were times with Curt's daughters, Danielle and Caroline, when Joyce would lose herself in the conversations the three of them had on the music they liked, on the movies they watched, on the arbitrarily delicate inner lives of young girls, and a crushing sense of doom would flatten her lungs as Jun-sang's little voice would call to her—*Halmeoni! Halmeoni!*—and she'd wonder if she'd ever have anything resembling what she had with her granddaughters. Struggling with Jung-sang in her halted, mannered Korean, asking Garrett to translate the words she was saying, made her feel like a tourist, until Jun-sang went off to play and they were left with nothing to discuss, other than Curt's trouble dealing with his girls.

That Joo-hee seemed noncommittal on Jun-sang learning English only made Joyce resent her even more. In moments that should've brought her more shame than she'd actually felt, Joyce would find herself thinking about Garrett's female friends from high school or college, wondering how life could have been had Garrett found a way to settle down with one of them instead. He could have stayed home, maybe moved to San Francisco or San Jose, had children named Cody or Jacob who called her *Nanna* or *Granny*. Maybe that wife could've had a better relationship with her own parents. Maybe Joyce and Garrett's in-laws would have had a friendly relationship, texting photos of Cody or Jacob to one another depending on which grandparents the boy was staying with at the given moment. Maybe that wife wouldn't have viewed her husband's relationship with his own mother as some vestigial tail. Maybe then, she wouldn't have asked herself if she should feel more shame than she was feeling. Maybe then, she wouldn't have tried to convince herself it wasn't racist to feel the way she did, that it had nothing to do with Joo-hee, or Korea, wouldn't have tried to convince herself that her favorite of Garrett's ex-girlfriends was the oustpoken Hispanic girl from Anaheim who couldn't even muster the decency to groan silently while they screwed in his room all Thanksgiving break.

The week before Garrett came to visit, Joyce had run into old Lindsey *What's-her-name*, the twiggy little brunette Garrett had taken to prom, at Safeway. Joyce had never liked her, the way she'd sit on their living room couch with her hands wedged between Garrett's knees, the way she'd always tried to overpower the smell of cigarettes on her clothes with sweet, little girl perfume.

Mrs. Hurley? Hi, I don't know if you remember me, but—

Lindsey! Of course I remember. Lindsey . . . I'm sorry sweetheart, blanking on the last name. Something Irish right?

Oh, no worries. Doyle was my maiden name. It's Kim now.

. . . Kim as in Korean Kim?

Yes it is. My husband is, in fact, Korean. Well, by way of Salt Lake City.

Well isn't that something . . .

As Garrett and Joo-hee slept off the jet lag in his old room, Joyce fixed herself a cup of tea, thinking about how Jun-sang had sat silently on the drive from SFO to Sacramento, staring at the bumper to bumper traffic. She hadn't seen him in person since he was a week old, the last time she'd gone to visit Garrett. She'd gotten into a fight with Joo-hee. It had been over Nancy, who hadn't been able to come with her. At this point, Joo-hee had already reunited with her birth mother, and Nancy had already told Joyce she couldn't bear to be in the same room with that woman. She told Joo-hee of the tearful conversations she'd had with Nancy over the phone—she'd even gone to Target and spent $100 on baby clothes, telling Joo-hee Nancy had sent them along with her. Nancy had begged Joyce not to do it, and maybe she shouldn't have, but it was important that Joo-hee know Nancy still loved her, that she still had a mother all the way in San Diego who missed her and thought about her every day.

You know this means they're never coming back, don't you?

Couldn't you just call her? Joyce had asked.

Please stop asking, Joo-hee had said.

They found each other here.

When Joo-hee's biological mother discovered Joyce's meddling, Joyce was sent to stay in a hotel, and for the rest of her trip, she held her grandson in her hotel room while Garrett and Joo-hee watched the rush hour commute on the streets below.

They belong here now.

We're never going to see them again.

As she took her tea into the living room, Joyce found Jun-sang sitting on the stairs. She asked him if he was doing well, if he was having trouble sleeping, and then realized she was speaking to him in the formal language she'd learned from her Korean language CDs and not the familiar language used with family—she could only speak to her grandson the way she might speak to an adult, a stranger at that—so she took his hand and brought him downstairs. They turned on the television. *The Force Awakens* was on TNT.

Su-ta Woh-ju, Jun-sang said.

Yes, Joyce smiled. *Star Wars*.

He pointed at the screen, said *Paseuma*. Joyce told him she didn't understand what that meant, and it wasn't until one of the other characters said Phasma, that she realized he was calling the villain by her name.

Do you enjoy *Star Wars*? Joyce asked in formal Korean, and the boy nodded, so she took him by the hand and they ran up to Curt's room. She sat him on the bed and told him to wait, while she ran into the kitchen to grab some Oreos.

They rummaged Curt's old toybox, pulling out every Star Wars action figure he'd owned—Joyce was convinced he'd owned every Star Wars toy every made—and she held up individual action figures while he named them for her: Han Solo, *Luku* Skywalker (So far so good), Darth Vader (*Dasseu Beido*), Leia (*Gongju*—princess! She knew that word!). They played for hours, only stopping to go downstairs and make turkey sandwiches, Curt's old bed covered in droids, and bounty hunters, and rebel pilots.

Joyce sat at the dining room table, the same table she'd spent fighting with Garrett before he'd finally moved to Korea, blissful for the first time since knowing they were coming to visit. Jun-sang alternated between bites of his sandwich and setting up Stormtroopers for Luke to knock down.

These toys belonged to your uncle Curt, she said in English. I wish he'd come see you, but he and your dad had a huge fight.

She felt a momentary burst of sadness as she imagined Nancy sitting with her, the two of them smiling as their grandson smiled at the table, Luke Skywalker facing off against a legion of Storm Troopers.

Poseureul iyonghaera, Jun-sang shouted as he banged the table.

The troopers fell over like dominoes. He set them up again.

I really hope he comes to his senses, Joyce said, mostly to herself. I'd love for you to meet him. Your dad never liked *Star Wars,* and Curt has little girls who think it's weird that he still loves this stuff. He'd probably love to play with you.

Poseureul iyonghaera, he shouted again, before banging the table.

I'm sorry, Sweetie, I don't know what you're saying.

He's saying, *Use the Force*.

Joyce turned to see Joo-hee walk into the kitchen. She asked if she could have some coffee, and Joyce told her to help herself, that this was her home too. Joo-hee poured herself a cup from the Mr. Coffee, the mug emblazoned with Yi Sun-sin Joyce had purchased in a gift shop with Nancy, and took a seat. Jun-sang tried to crawl into her lap until her mother told her the coffee was hot. To Joyce's amazement, the boy leapt into her lap instead. She placed her chin on the crown of her grandson's head.

I see he's shown you his *Star Wars* expertise, Joo-hee said.

It's so strange, Joyce said. Garrett hated *Star Wars*.

He gets it from me, Joo-hee smiled. I used to watch it with my dad all the time.

Oh, that's nice. Don't you miss him? Don't you miss your mother?

Joo-hee slurped her coffee. Jun-sang held two Snowtroopers aloft, made shooting sounds. He held them out for his mother. She smiled as she took one and posed its arms and legs.

Let's not do this, Joyce. Please, I just want to have a nice trip.

When Garrett was eight, Joyce read him the story of the Monkey's Paw because he'd asked for a scary story, and it was two nights before Halloween. A man with a magical monkey's paw wishes for money to pay off his mortgage, in spite of warnings to not tempt fate. The next day, his son dies in a workplace accident, and the company gives the man a settlement in the exact amount of the mortgage. When Garrett asked why the son had to die, Joyce told him it was because the paw was cursed—that while it granted your every wish, doing so came at a price, so the paw granted his wish for the money, but took his son in exchange. Garrett became so upset he begged her to stop reading the story, cried at its cruelty, so Joyce stopped and instead read the story of Dick Whittington and his cat.

And every time Joyce received an email, or a card, or a video call from Garrett, she couldn't help but think of the story she'd never finished reading, how the man's wife wished for their son to return from the dead, in spite of his premonitions the boy would come back as a rotting corpse, forcing the man to use their final wish to send their son back to the realm of the dead.

Three days after the incident in the seafood restaurant, Garrett showered and came down to the kitchen. Joyce turned from the sink and smiled. Her heart raced—it had been the first time he'd left his room since that night. Garrett poured a cup of coffee and stared into the mug, the steam wisping upward until fading away. Joyce asked him if he'd like some eggs.

There's this program, he said. It helps adoptees relocate to Korea and readjust to the culture. It teaches us to be Koreans again.

I don't understand.

This isn't about you or Curt. I love you both. You have to know that.

But you're not Korean, Garrett. You're an American boy.

She repeated the phrase, *You're an American boy*, knowing the added emphasis wasn't going to change anything. Garrett reached out, placed his hand on her wrist, ran his thumb along the back of her hand.

Mom, it doesn't have to be like this.

Garrett removed his hand from hers, sipped his coffee.

You remember when I stopped you from reading "The Monkey's Paw" to me? Garrett asked.

You mean the worst Halloween ever?

He laughed, and she laughed. It was a small comfort in the midst of losing her son.

That night, after you went to sleep, I went to Curt's room because I had to know how it all turned out. He told me the ending, how the husband wished the zombie son away. I got really freaked out and couldn't stop thinking about what people would be like when they came back from the dead.

You were always easily scared.

Yeah. I really was. Anyway, I didn't sleep well for the next few nights. I mean, I was exhausted on Halloween if you remember. The reason I didn't sleep was because I'd spent months wishing for Dad to come back, and now I was scared that he might.

Oh, Garrett. I'm so sorry.

I just had these horrible thoughts of Dad coming back into the house, the skin peeling from his skull, his clothes covered in dirt and leaves.

Joyce stood and walked over to him, put her arms around his head, pulled him into her stomach. There was a tightness to him, as if he were trying to remember how to react toward her affection, how to pose while being held.

And so I started wishing for him to stay dead, he said. And I felt so guilty about that. Can you imagine, wishing for someone to stay dead?

Garrett loosened her grip, kissed her hands. He stood up and made his way toward the Mr. Coffee for another cup.

When I was in Iraq, he said. I had this dream. I only had it once, but I couldn't stop thinking about it. I'd come home, dressed in my fatigues. Everyone stared at me from their yards and they all looked so sad, but I didn't care because I was home. I ran up the porch, really excited to see all of you, but the door was locked, so I jiggled the knob a couple times, and then started banging on the door because I finally realized something was wrong. Then I heard Dad on the other side of the door saying, *You wished me away, so I wished you away. You're the dead one now. You're the dead one.*

Dad would never wish you away, Joyce said. Neither would I.

I know, Mom. I know that.

Danielle and Caroline, Curt's daughters, came through the door with Pookie, their Australian Sheepdog. Joyce hugged them as Pookie ran up to Jun-sang and began licking. As Garrett marveled at how big they were, Joyce walked out the door and into the driveway, where Curt was waiting with the engine running.

Hi Mom. The girls wanted to see their uncle.

You coming in?

Maybe later. I have to go to the driving range.

Now?

It's a client. He wants to go hit some balls.

You should go see your nephew. He's really something. He likes *Star Wars*, just like you. Where's Anna?

Book club. She says she'll stop by later tonight.

Will you be joining us too?

Glad he's home.

He handed her two one-hundred dollar bills, asked her to buy Jun-sang some nice toys. When she suggested Curt take his nephew himself, he told her he loved her and backed out of the driveway. Joyce walked over to Garrett, who was on the porch in his socks. Curt waved and Garrett nodded. She held Garrett's hand as Curt drove off.

He'll come around, Joyce said.

Joyce had always wanted for her sons to be closer, but it was always hard to get the bookish Garrett and the more athletic Curt to ever agree on anything. The only time they'd ever gotten along was the month before Garrett went off to the Army, when they'd spent hours lifting weights together. Curt had been so proud of his little brother. He'd bragged about Garrett every time he saw another man in uniform, how he was so thankful there were so many good men out there to watch over his brother.

It seemed to Joyce Curt wasn't necessarily upset about Garrett going off to Korea—he'd even said it might be good for him to spend some time finding himself—it was more that Garrett had renounced his American citizenship. How the hell does a man do what he did and then turn his back on his country? And Curt's wife Anna wasn't much help, either. The night she'd heard about Garrett's plans, Anna suggested he should be more grateful that kind Americans like Joyce and Rich had pulled him out of poverty, and then the yelling began, and no amount of backtracking, no amount of apologies, could repair the damage she'd done.

Anna might stop by later tonight. Can you try to be nice?

Of course. You know me, Mom. I'm always the bigger person.

Garrett smiled. He kissed her on the head and made his way inside. Joyce turned and saw Jun-sang giggling as Caroline sat with her arms around him, Danielle tickling his little ribs. Joo-hee sat on the steps, petting Pookie, smiling as Garrett sat next to her, put his arm around her.

Two nights after Garrett had begged for Dick Whittington, Joyce took him Trick-or-Treating. He'd wanted to be Dracula, so she'd fashioned a silk cape with red lining and pressed his black pants and the white dress shirt he'd worn to her niece's wedding. He looked amazing with his black hair slicked back, white make-up caked to his face, the plastic fangs they'd purchased at Walgreens. She told him it was like looking at the face of Bela Lugosi himself, which confused him even after she'd explained who Bela Lugosi was. He asked if they could watch Bela Lugosi after they came home, and she promised him he could watch half—it was a school night, after all.

It was the first year Garrett had chosen not to wear a mask—having been some variation of Spider-Man, or Wolverine, or Batman every other Halloween—and Joyce was excited he'd chosen what she'd felt to be a Big Kid costume. They made their way through their block, the neighbors complimenting Garrett on his costume, giving him high fives, playfully shielding their necks with their hands. They were having a lovely night, and at the time she'd wished Curt hadn't decided he was too old to come with them, wished he hadn't chosen to sit around and play that stupid 007 video game with his friends.

It wasn't until they'd ventured past their block and up the hill that things turned sour. The first house they'd gone to, a man grinned and said, *All right! Chinese Dracula!* before dropping a fun-sized Milky Way into Garrett's pillowcase. As they left the house, Garrett asked why the man thought he was Chinese, and Joyce told him to ignore it.

Some kids at school think I'm Chinese too, Garrett had said.

Well, you're not, Joyce said.

At the third house, a man dressed like Clint Eastwood's Man with No Name—he was clearly drunk—told Garrett, *I've never seen an Asian vampire. I like it*, to which Garrett told him he was actually Dracula.

Sure you are, bud, the man slurred.

Their mailbox read GOLDBERG, and Joyce wanted to tell him she'd never seen a Jewish cowboy, either—but what good would that have done? Garrett and the man high-fived, and then she walked her son down the stairs, Garrett asking why she'd muttered, *Asshole*, under her breath.

As they made their way down the hill, Joyce couldn't get their words out of her head, the words of adults who should've known better:

Oh, you're Korean? My mistake, little buddy—Korean Dracula!

I saw a little boy who looked just like you dressed like a samurai. It was adorable. Maybe the two of you could be friends.

Hey kids, you all look fantastic. Here's a candy for Snow White, here's one for Frankenstein, one for the Ghostbuster, and one for my little Asian Dracula here.

Hey man, next year you should be a ninja. I bet you cold totally pull that off!

At the bottom of the hill, they decided to stop by one last house. An elderly woman was sitting on the porch with an overweight Golden Retriever dressed like an indolent bumblebee. Joyce breathed a momentary sigh of relief when the woman told Garrett how handsome he was in his Dracula outfit, but then she asked Garrett where he was from, to which Joyce coldly responded he was from down the street.

Oh I know that, the woman had said. I see him riding his bike all the time. He's so conscientious, the way he slows down at intersections and looks both ways. I just wanted to let his mother know what a good boy he is.

I am his mother, Joyce said. I'm his goddamn mother. If you want to tell him what a good boy he is, you tell me.

I didn't mean anything by it.

None of you ever do.

Joyce snatched Garrett by the hand and stormed off.

They got home and had pizza on the couch. She was too upset to yell at Curt for smelling like pot. They didn't get very far in the film, as the boys laughed the first time they saw Dracula. When Renfield cut his finger and Dracula hungrily approached the blood, they snickered.

When the crucifix dropped from Renfield's shirt and dangled in front of the cut finger, the boys howled with laughter as Dracula shielded his eyes with his cape.

I can't believe you wanted to dress like this asswipe, Curt said.

Let's watch our language around your brother, Joyce said.

I know, Garrett laughed. No one even got it. They thought I was some Chinese guy.

Joyce stopped the movie, and they watched a bowdlerized version of *Pet Sematary* on AMC until Garrett fell asleep on her lap. In spite of her objections, Garrett went as a ninja the following year because his friends said he looked cool. And the year after that, Garrett asked if he could stay home with Curt and hand out candy, meaning Garrett sat on the porch and handed out candy while Curt smoked a joint in the garage. He would never Trick-or-Treat again.

It warmed Joyce's heart to see how famously Joo-hee got along with the girls, the way Caroline and Danielle doted on their little cousin. She leaned against the kitchen sink and listened to their laughter, the banter between her granddaughters and her daughter-in-law, and couldn't help but smile as she checked her phone for messages. She took a sip of water and prepared herself. Things were going so well. Everyone was in a fantastic mood. How could things not work out?

She put her phone away as soon as Garrett walked into the kitchen. He grabbed a tumbler from the cabinet.

It's too bad your brother couldn't stay, she said.

It is what it is, Mom.

Could you maybe be a little more broken up about it?

The icemaker hummed, pellets of oblong ice clinking into the tumbler. Garret poured himself a glass of water and shook his head. She wanted to tell him he shouldn't dismiss his brother so easily, to give him a little credit, wanted to tell him how badly Curt wanted to be a good uncle, how he saw it as a way to mend fences with Garrett and Joo-hee, how Curt had Jun-sang's baby pictures all over his fridge. Garrett chugged his water and exhaled.

He and I talked about me coming down, he said. Things were going fine until he mentioned how much you wanted Joo-hee to reconnect with her mom and dad. It got pretty heated. And it's fine he did that. He only wanted to make you happy. I told him it wasn't going to happen, but he wouldn't let it go.

I don't know about that, Joyce said. Maybe we need to give Joo-hee's folks a little more credit. The fact that you're both here makes me really hopeful.

Do you know why my wife doesn't want to see her family? Garrett asked. It's because of me. Her dad said marrying me was proof she wasn't coming home and he kind of shut down after that. He told her he'd always hoped she'd meet some American guy in Korea, some soldier or English teacher who'd help her come to her senses and bring her home. Can you believe that?

You know this means they're never coming back, don't you?

They found each other here.

Her dad doesn't want to see her, ever. And it's because of me. If she'd married some white guy, he might've been okay with it. But the fact that it was me was what did him in. He told her that he'd put up with everything, but if she married me it was over between them. She's dead to him, that's what he said, Mom. She's dead to him, and he's dead to her.

They belong here now.

We're never seeing them again.

Joyce leaned against the counter, closed her eyes and took deep breaths. Garrett asked if she was okay, told her she was scaring him, begged her to tell him what was wrong. Joo-hee came into the kitchen, asked if everything was okay. She placed her hand on Joyce's shoulder, and Joyce looked into Joo-hee's face, stroked her cheek, told her she was so sorry, and Joo-hee shifted her eyes toward Garrett.

What's going on? she asked.

They're coming to my house, Joyce whispered.

Who's coming, Mom? Garrett asked. Who?

Joyce began to gasp and wheeze. Joo-hee put her arm around her waist. She stroked Joyce's hair, called for the girls, who ran in and took their grandmother's hands, imploring her to calm down, to breathe, told her she wasn't an idiot, begged her to stop crying. Her phone buzzed and chimed in her back pocket. Caroline told her not to worry about it, that she could call them back.

The doorbell rang, and everyone stopped and turned—a man's voice, and then a woman's, through the screen door, calling out for someone named Emily.

The Ruins

PETE WELLIGER was the giant asshole who owned Shared Universe Comics, the only comic store within a thirty-mile radius. He ran a blog where he bragged about what a great businessman he was, gave tips on how to make money selling comic books, and posted pictures of himself rock climbing in superhero T-shirts, or paddle boarding with beautiful women, with captions that read "In the temple of his spirit, each man is alone," or "The question isn't who is going to let me; it's who is going to stop me." He was full of himself, but he wasn't wrong—he really was a great businessman, who'd gotten rich selling commercial real estate before taking over the empty space that was once a Blockbuster Video, a space that had only been used once a year for the previous six years as a Halloween outlet store until he set up shop and ran his competitors out of business. I used to go to Shared Universe every Wednesday to buy comics and ask if he had any job openings, and he'd always tell me he respected my initiative and remind me he had my application on file.

During my junior year of high school, Shared Universe hosted a contest sponsored by a local talk radio host named Gordy French. Contestants were asked to draw a picture of the prophet Muhammed, which was forbidden—due to Muhammed being a man, and being depicted in a drawing could lead to idol worship—which I know now, but didn't then. Welliger's decision to host the contest wasn't something that just angered comic bloggers and artists, the national media picked up on it as well. Welliger said he was doing it in honor of all the cartoonists who'd been threatened for drawing Muhammed, that he was doing it in the name of free speech. An editor at Marvel Comics supposedly vowed to blacklist any artist who took part in the contest, but then denied saying that when accused of censorship.

I only entered that contest because Bruce Murphy, one of my heroes, was going to judge. Murphy's *The White Devil Rides Again* is the greatest graphic novel of all time, and I know a lot of people look down on him now because of his politics, but what he did in that comic was real-life stuff. Every punch thrown had the grace and power of a bullet from a gun. Every tensed muscle was drawn by a man who knew what it felt like to have your back against the wall. And every woman looked like the kind of woman a man would risk death for. He was the real deal, and if he was involved then so was I. All my friends begged me not to do it, that it wasn't going to be worth the hassle, but having the opportunity to showcase my work to Bruce Murphy was going to be a dream come true—back when I actually thought dreams came true.

The parking lot outside of Shared Universe was a madhouse. Cops were shoving back the line of angry protesters, with their *two, four, six, eight*'s, and *hey-hey, ho-ho*'s. Behind the cops, on the sidewalk in front of the store, stood a row of bikers from a gang called the Legion of Blood. I remembered seeing their leader on TV, talking about how they were going to make sure everyone's First Amendment rights were protected, by any means necessary. The news reporter asked their leader about their history of violence and he said they only acted in self-defense, and when the reporter asked about their name, he said it meant brotherhood and wasn't a celebration of violence. That made me feel a little better about going, that maybe these guys weren't as bad as the news was making them sound.

In spite of what a lot of people think, I did struggle with whether I should take part in the contest—I really did. But all I wanted in life was to draw comics. Drawing comics helped convince me that my life wasn't a hole I couldn't crawl out of—it was actually a tunnel, and all I had to do was make it to the other side. Because my parents were Buddhist, and not Methodist like every other Korean in town, I heard a lot about how life was suffering but there was an end to the suffering, and for me, comics were that end. I used to imagine I was this lone traveler wandering through a post-apocalypse. Every once in a while, I'd have to deal with roving bandits or gangs of mutants, but I knew I'd one day get to the promised land, and once I was there, I'd raise an army, and we'd go back and clean up the rest of the world, rebuild it into something better, so wanderers like me wouldn't have to fear for their lives every time they took their journey. I'd always thought I was better than what people thought of me, that the world was probably even better than I thought it was, and comics were going to be the key to proving that. I never wanted to hurt anyone, and I didn't want anyone to hurt me either—so when Mrs. Turlock, who was my English teacher during freshman year, shouted, Shame on you, James Chae, from behind the wall of cops, I had to shut my eyes, knowing I couldn't ever shut my ears.

You should know better, she yelled.

A biker clapped my shoulder, and I almost buckled from the pressure.

Don't worry about them, brother, the biker said. Standing up for what's right is what men do.

And I thanked him because I believed him.

Gordy French shook my hand as soon as I walked in, said it was nice to see a young person who cared about freedom of expression. He was shorter than I thought he'd be, because his radio voice was so deep, and dressed in a long-sleeved Aloha shirt and brown slacks. Standing next to him was Pete Welliger, who chucked my shoulder like we were old friends. I hated French's show. All he did was yell at people, and everyone who called in was an idiot. I told him my parents were fans, and he told me to hug my mother for him. He always had nice things to say about Asians, how hard-working we were, how we kept our noses clean, probably because his wife was Asian—which he told me for no reason.

James is a very talented comic artist, Welliger said.

Then he's in the right place, French said.

I asked if Bruce Murphy was here yet, and they said he was in the back office conducting a radio interview. French told me to take a seat in front of one of the easels and Murphy would come around and introduce himself. They promised I'd get V.I.P treatment, which I can't say I remember getting, and then Welliger offered to personally walk me to an easel, and French said that was a great idea. He shook my hand one more time, thanking me for giving him hope for the future. Welliger put his hand on my shoulder and told me to walk with him. There were three rows of six easels, each holding giant white sheets of paper. I told him I was more comfortable drawing on a table.

Do you know what integrity is, James? he asked. It's the ability to stand by an idea.

I told him I remembered that quote. It was on the homepage of his blog, next to the photo of him—shirtless, hitting a giant tire with a sledgehammer.

It's from a wonderful book called *The Fountainhead,* he said. Ever read it?

I told him I hadn't, and he said to stop by the store later this week when I had time and he'd give me a copy, said every serious artist should read it, that it happened to be Bruce Murphy's favorite book. He also said I'd get a 20% discount on whatever I bought that day. We stopped in front of my drawing station. Welliger smiled, put his hand on my back.

James, my man, he said, it took a lot of courage to come here.

Thanks, Mr. Welliger.

James, you've always had the ability to call me Pete. You just never took advantage of it.

Okay. Thanks, Pete.

I'm gonna head back over with Gordy. Now let's turn the page.

I set my backpack on the floor and took a seat, watched him walk away. Welliger always signed off his blog posts with, Let's turn the page—an obvious rip-off of Stan Lee's *Excelsior!* sign-off. It made me think of my favorite scene in Bruce Murphy's *The White Devil Rides Again*, when the White Devil speeds through the rainy streets on his HellCycle, thinking about his destiny. He has an interior monologue about how some men think turning the page is all it takes to move on, but he knows better because he was a crime reporter long before he was a vigilante. He knows he can't forget the things he sees, can't unsee the things he wants to forget. Other men can't see the blood on the page the way he can, and that's why they turn the page. The White Devil vows to show all men the blood, to make sure they'll never forget. I recited the entire monologue in my head—visualized each panel, each shot, where each caption was placed—while I stared at the blank page in front of me.

I'd already had everything planned out, even done a mock-up be-cause I couldn't sleep. My version of Muhammed was an intergalactic tyrant, like Darkseid from the Justice League, an armored colossus with a thick beard like the ones worn by the Legion of Blood, but his beard was the jet black void of outer space—you could literally see stars and planets in it. His right hand, an iron fist clutching a tattered American flag. His left hand, a glowing scimitar. He stood atop flam-ing sand dunes, teeth bared, eyes emitting bolts of energy. I was so excited to get drawing, to show it to Bruce Murphy, to win this stupid contest and really get my life in gear.

I turned to the guy on my left , an old man with a handlebar mus-tache, and said hello. He said his name was Jim, so I told him my name was James too. He laughed and said we were practically related. We shook hands. He was one of those guys who shook your hand with both of his, seemed really warm and friendly like the kind of person who'd show you pictures of his grand-daughters—which he did. I then turned to the guy on my right and said hello. The left side of his face was scarred, like Cable from the X-Men. He smiled and nodded, and then went back to staring at the blank page.

Murphy finally came out of the back room—black blazer, black dress shirt, black jeans, and gray fedora. He stopped and shook hands with each of us. I told him he was one of my heroes and he smiled, said it was nice to hear. He asked the scarred guy next to me, who said his name was Jeff, if he was in the military. Jeff said he was, and Murphy thanked him for his service and walked toward Welliger and French, who stood with their arms crossed behind the glass counter.

Only sixteen people entered the contest, and besides me, there was only one real artist in the bunch, the scary-looking guy who sat next to me. Calling him scary seems like a funny thing to say, seeing how almost half the people in the contest were from the Legion of Blood, but Jeff really was scary with his shaved head and muscles rippling through his tight red T-shirt. Jeff actually looked like a comic book character, as if every shirt he wore highlighted his physique. He didn't talk much, just stared really hard, but I knew he was in the Marines because of the USMC insignia tattooed on his left arm. I also knew he'd been drinking because he smelled like the jocks who harassed me during my evening shifts at Jack in the Box. He turned to me, and I realized I was staring at the scar that ran down his left eye, so I turned away.

Ahnyoung haseyo, he said.

How did you know I was Korean?

Because you are, he said. What's your name, man?

James.

THIS IS THE AFTERLIFE

He shook my hand, which hurt my hand a little, and I asked him if he was a Bruce Murphy fan and he told me he thought he was okay, that he liked the earlier stuff way more, thought the White Devil was over-rated. So I asked him why he was here then, and he shrugged and said his mom wanted him out of the house. I wanted to ask him why a grown man like him would still be living with his mom but wisely chose not to.

What's your story, James?

He must've realized I didn't know what he meant by that because he kept going, asking me what brought me here, what I was hoping to accomplish, so I told him I wanted to draw something that Bruce Murphy might like, and that maybe this would help me kickstart my comic book career. He said that sounded promising, and for some reason I believed him, so I started telling him about my comic before a biker came over and leaned in between us.

Gentlemen, he said, the name's Dennis. My friends call me Dennis the Menace. So you better call me Dennis the Menace

I'm James, and this is Jeff.

Dennis told me he was going to call me Rush Hour and nudged me on the shoulder. He then laughed and told me he was just fucking with me. For some reason, it was different from when the kids at school called me Jackie Chan, even though it was basically the same thing. He had long stringy hair and a bushy beard, like most of the other bikers in the room, but he looked different from them—maybe it was because he was smiling, maybe it was because he was fucking with me, just fucking with me, that is.

Listen, he said, I'm here drawing like the rest of you but I'm also here to provide security. So if any of those assholes outside give you trouble, you call your boy Dennis the Menace. Got it?

Jeff said nothing, so I thanked Dennis. He nodded and told me to call him Dennis the Menace, and then slapped me on the back a little too hard before he walked over to Jim.

How's life, old-timer? The name's Dennis the Menace.

I heard you, Dennis, Jim said.

Jeff pulled a flask from the backpack at his feet, took a sip. Welliger leaned over the glass counter and shouted there was no drinking in the store. A biker sitting two rows ahead of us, a tall lanky guy with black braided pigtails like a Native American, turned around. I'd find out later his name was Chavo.

What you got in there, Pretty Boy? he asked.

Jeff leaned over and asked the elderly lady sitting in front of us to pass the flask to Chavo. She refused, so Chavo walked over to us and grabbed the flask. I decided I didn't like this woman, who was wearing a T-shirt with Calvin pissing on an *Obama 2008* sign. Welliger once again asked that we not drink in the store, but French held up an open palm and asked Welliger to calm down. Chavo took a swig and handed it back to Jeff.

Thanks, brother, he said.

Chavo walked back to his station, and the old lady sitting in front of us screwed up her face and shook her head.

Please put that away, Welliger shouted.

Aw, let 'em have their fun, Pete. French said. The man's a damn war hero, for Christ's sake.

Jeff then offered the flask to Jim, who looked at it and smiled a sad smile. He stroked his mustache and shook his head.

Thanks, son, Jim said, but I haven't had a drink since my first grand-daughter was born.

How long ago was that? Jeff asked.

Twelve years.

Jim put his hand on my shoulder, shook it gently. Jeff looked past me, over my shoulder, and I wanted to know what Jim was doing. Did he look angry? Was he even returning Jeff's gaze? Was he averting his eyes, staring at me?

I admire that, Jeff said. I really do.

Best decision I ever made in my life, Jim said. You ever want to quit, I'll buy you a cup of coffee and we can talk.

Thank you, sir. I'll keep it under consideration.

Please do.

Jim kept his hand on my shoulder and leaned in, advised me not to go sneaking sips of *that stuff*, as he called it. I told him I wouldn't and he told me I was a good man. I looked to the counter, and Welliger looked at me, threw his hands up as if pleading his case. Murphy pointed at me, finger-guns, and winked.

I'd already sketched everything out and moved on to inking, but Jeff hadn't even picked up a pencil. He just stared at the blank sheet of paper in front of him, sneaking a drink every once in a while. I noticed Bruce Murphy never walked around to look at the artwork, which was something I was looking forward to. That was supposed to be my chance to strike up a conversation with him.

So what are you drawing, James? he'd ask.

This is how I see Muhammed, I'd say. He's an intergalactic tyrant who comes to our planet in order to enslave us.

That's not bad, he'd say. Tell me more.

And then I'd tell him about *PryM8*, my comic about a homeless veteran who had the ability to transform into a cybernetic ape from another dimension, except he didn't really transform into the ape. An accident in a secret lab cursed him to travel to another dimension where ape-like beings were enslaved by blue humanoids. While the homeless soldier was wandering through the battle-scarred wasteland, assembling an ape army to liberate their world from mutated apes and the blue humanoids, Subject #8, an ape from the enslaved planet, wandered the streets of New York fighting for the homeless who were being murdered by corrupt cops, superhuman mercenaries, and greedy businessmen. Both characters were powerless in their own worlds, but became heroes once they traded places.

That's a hell of a drawing, James, Jeff said.

Thanks, I said. It's Muhammed. At least how I see him.

It's really cool.

You think so?

Shit, man, if me and my friends had run into this guy I'd have more than just this scar.

He smiled and gestured toward the scar that ran down his left eye. I felt bad, as if I'd somehow reminded him he had a giant scar on his face. It looked like a mountain range on a relief map. The raised, pink skin puckered like a rotting apple.

So what're you drawing? I asked.

He shrugged and said he wasn't even sure if he was going to draw anything at all. I asked him if he even liked drawing and he said he used to love it, but stopped drawing in Afghanistan and never went back. He told me he was only here because his mother wanted him to draw again, even though he really didn't care anymore.

But why not just take an art class or something? I asked.

My mom's crazy, he laughed. Like all these people. I guess she thought maybe it would inspire me.

He peered over at what Pissing Calvin Lady was drawing and motioned for me to look, a giant eagle grasping a sandaled foot in its talons. She hadn't finished drawing Muhammed yet, but I could already picture him dangling upside down in the eagle's grasp. Terrible composition—one of the wings was clearly shorter than the other and there was no sense of movement in the pantleg she'd begun working on. The blood from Muhammed's ankle geysered upward, which made no sense because the eagle was soaring toward the left of the page. No sense of movement at all. At the very least, she could've added some speedlines. She turned around and caught us, sneered.

Worry about your own damn drawings, she said.

The lady's right fellas, Jim said. Leave her be.

Jeff asked me if I knew who Ralph Steadman was, and then asked if I was kidding when I said no. He pulled a hardcover from his backpack, a book of Steadman drawings. I told him it reminded me of Bruce Murphy, and he laughed and said I was hopeless.

What was it like? I asked. Being in Afghanistan, I mean.

Jeff shrugged, and said he didn't know, which I thought was weird—of course he knew—but that was all I got. Murphy paced behind the glass counter, turned and stared at the wall of bagged and boarded silver age comics and vintage action figures on the wall behind the counter. He untacked the the copy of *Tales of Suspense* #50 hanging from the wall and took it out of its bag—this is a comic from 1964—and began flipping through it, while a clearly nervous Welliger watched him.

This isn't really Muhammed, I said. It's a character from my comic. I've been working on it for like three years.

Yeah man, Jeff said. It shows. Not that it isn't Muhammed, but that you put a lot of thought into it.

He asked me who it really was, and I told him it was Bronn Shang, the tyrant of Dimension 443X, an alternate timeline in which apes didn't evolve into men but gained consciousness themselves. I told him how Bronn Shang's race enslaved the apes of Earth 443X and performed cruel experiments on Subject #8, turning him into a machine in an attempt to kill his soul. I told him about Sgt. Brock Primus, Special Forces, who was the subject of a government test that left him mentally unstable, but also turned his body into a dimensional portal. Then I felt bad. I didn't want him to think I saw all veterans as mentally disturbed.

So this Primus guy and Ape-8 switch places? Jeff asked.

Subject #8, I said. And yeah, Primus goes to Earth 443X and Subject #8 comes to our Earth, where they're both given new purpose. Until the portal wears off, anyway, and Primus goes back to being homeless and crazy, and Subject #8 goes back to the lab where they torture him.

Why did I say crazy? I thought. I swear, I wanted to tell him. I don't think all veterans are crazy.

But they remember what they did when they switched places, I said. So, you know, that keeps them going.

Dreams of a better world, Jeff said. I like it. It's really cool, man. Make sure to tell Murphy about your comic.

You think he'll like it?

Unless he's some kind of retard, yeah. It's really good.

Jeff bent over and pulled his flask from the backpack, took another sip. I looked over at Welliger, whose cheeks puffed out as he shook his head. Murphy looked up from the comic, first at Welliger, then at me. He chuckled and went back to reading. Jeff stood up, put the flask in his back pocket. He turned to the three men at the cash register.

I'm gonna take a smoke break, he said.

Before Welliger could object, Murphy said that was a good idea and asked if he could bum one. Dennis the Menace said he'd go out with them to make sure there wasn't any trouble. Welliger's lips tightened. He exhaled through his nose.

Use the back entrance, he said. There's no one next to the dumpsters.

Chavo stood up, and then all the bikers stood up. Jeff asked me if I wanted to go, said it was my chance to tell Murphy about my comic. I stayed and drew. It wasn't until everyone left that I realized how loud the store had been. Without the bikers laughing and joking around, I could hear the protesters outside, really focus on what they were saying. A woman kept screaming *U-S-A, U-S-A*, over and over again, and the protesters began to boo. She was so consistent and shrill—it was hard not to hear her over everyone else. Every once in a while, she'd punctuate her U-S-A chant with a *Woooo!* to let us know how excited she was. I wondered if Mrs. Turlock was still out there. She'd always been nice to me, even when other teachers always weren't. I'd even lent her my copy of *Watchmen*, which she told me was beautifully written. She showed me two poems, "The Tyger" and "Ozymandias," to show me how they fit into the comic. I had no idea Ozymandias was a poem. It took everything I had to focus on drawing again, to shut everyone out.

U-S-A, U-S-A, U-S-A, U-S-A. Wooooooo!

I looked around the empty room. There were only eight of us left. Pissing Calvin Lady hadn't made much progress. Chavo's drawing was terrible: a bearded man in a turban with a knife in his head, x's for eyes. The man had a giant nose like a toucan's beak. It was so typical and stupid. None of them were taking this seriously.

Shameful, isn't it? said Jim.

What do you mean?

These people. None of them have a lick of talent, not like you. No sense of principle, either. They're just here to cause trouble and have a laugh.

I asked if I could see his drawing: a bearded man in a turban, standing behind a burning Bible, holding the Constitution over the flames. It wasn't great, but it wasn't terrible, either.

So what brings you here, Jim? Are you trying to win that prize money for your grandkids?

Heck no, he said. Sure, it'll all go to them, but that's not why I'm here. I'm an artist James. Just like you, just like that drunk you've taken a shine to. And I'm not gonna let some camel-fucking blasphemers tell me what I can and can't draw in my own damn country.

I decided I wasn't going to talk to Jim anymore.

When Jeff finally came back, Dennis the Menace had his arm around his shoulder. Jeff stared at me, and I could tell he was really uncomfortable with Dennis—not scared of Dennis, more annoyed, like he wanted to be left alone. Jeff took a seat, and Dennis leaned over my shoulder. I could smell the cigarettes and whiskey.

Let's see what we got here, he said. Jesus Christ, this is really good, man.

Thanks.

Captain Logan here told us you're working on a comic.

I looked over to Jeff, who was putting his flask away. His last name was Logan? Like Wolverine? I didn't know he was a Captain. I don't even know why that mattered. I was furious he'd told them about my comic, that he'd told Murphy before I could. I prayed he didn't tell him Bronn Shang wasn't really Muhammed.

What? I said. Why?

Because he believes in you, dumbass—that's why. I think it's really great, man. You keep this up, Rush Hour. Don't ever quit, you hear me? You can do whatever the hell you want in life, man. Don't ever forget that.

Thanks, Dennis.

C'mon, Rush Hour, he said, you can call me Dennis the Menace.

His name's James, Jeff said.

Hey relax, Cap, Dennis said. You'll live longer. Just messing with the kid. You know I like you, don't you—James?

I looked over at Jeff, who was finally drawing. He was slashing at the page with a Sharpie, real broad strokes, and I could tell he knew exactly what he was doing. His body didn't move at all, just his right arm. The Sharpie squeaked against the paper and, all of the sudden, I didn't feel like the best artist in the room anymore. It was like he wasn't staring at the page, but staring into it. I don't think I've ever been in the place he was in that moment. It all seemed so mysterious and it made me jealous.

Well, better get back to work, Dennis said. Good job, James. Proud of you, bud. Captain Jeffrey Logan, it was a pleasure, Captain, sir.

Dennis gave a sarcastic salute and left. Jeff didn't look up once. I got back to my drawing and the violent swish of Jeff's Sharpie slowly disappeared into the sounds of laughter and locker room talk—the room was finally loud again. Pissing Calvin Lady groaned.

Did you really tell Bruce Murphy about my comic? I asked.

Don't worry, Jeff said. I didn't tell him that wasn't really Muhammed.

Did he seem interested?

You'll have to talk to him about it. He says we have about forty-five minutes left. You better get going.

So your last name is Logan? I asked.

Yes, James. My last name is Logan like fucking Wolverine, okay?

He swatted my arm with the back of his hand and laughed—we both did. Then he got back to drawing, and Pissing Calvin Lady asked everyone to keep it down. I stood up, stretched my legs. I looked out the window, the sea of snarling faces. Mrs. Turlock was gone. For the rest of the year, I made sure not to walk past Mrs. Turlock's classroom, taking the long way to every class I had in that hallway. It wasn't that much of a big deal. Wherever you went, the whole place was a giant shithole anyway.

When we did pass each other, she never said hi, never even looked at me. I can't say I blame her too much.

French called time and asked us to put our pencils down. If I'd had ten more minutes I might have been able to finish shading it in. There were a lot of flaws showing because I hadn't had time to color in the shadows. Fifteen more minutes—maybe twenty—that was all I needed. Then it would've been perfect. Murphy, Welliger, and French began making their rounds—Welliger did the first row, French did the second, and Murphy came to ours. Jeff put his pen down.

I don't even know how he had the time to finish the drawing, but it was amazing. Five soldiers dressed for desert warfare, their faces grimy from battle, all looking down at something. They were like trees towering over us, rifles slung over their shoulders. Flecks of red ink spattered across the left side of the page—it was beautiful, and sad, and scary, and had nothing to do with what the contest was supposed to be about.

Holy crap, man, I said. This is really good.

Thanks, man.

But what does this have to do with Muhammed?

It's just what came out.

The others gathered around to take a look—Murphy, Welliger, and French. They began discussing things I couldn't hear. All I know is French looked confused and Welliger was pissed.

So what's going on here? Murphy asked.

Well, Jeff said, this guy here, that's Lance Corporal Davidson. This one's PFC Greene. This one's Lance Corporal Jackson—Ray Jax. This is Snead. And that's Sergeant Jones.

So you know these guys? Murphy asked.

They were my Rifle Company.

Okay, Welliger said, but what does this have to do with Muhammed?

Jeff looked Welliger dead in the eye. Welliger turned away and I saw the rage on his face, the wasted time, the fact that he'd let a drunk into his store. Jeff turned back to his drawing, just stared at it. The guy they called Ray Jax looked a little scared, like he was trying not to cry. The others looked kind of like they were trying to be brave in the face of danger, like they knew if one of them faltered, the others might as well.

I see you're a Ralph Steadman fan, Murphy said. You and I speak the same language. Did you really do all this with a Sharpie?

Everyone came over and gathered around the picture, began talking amongst themselves, saying things like, What is this, and How is this Muhammed, and What the fuck is this guy trying to say, and the like. Chavo finally spoke up.

Hey man, you trying to say that our soldiers are like Muhammed? Please tell me that's not what you're saying. Please tell me that's not what you're fucking saying.

They're not soldiers, Jeff said. They're Marines.

Chavo told Jeff they should step outside, and Dennis the Menace pulled him away. Dennis looked at me and winked, gave me a thumbs up to let me know everything was cool. French asked the men to calm down.

I have to agree with the gentleman who just spoke, Welliger said. Is that what you're saying? Are these men Muhammed?

Do they look like Muhammed? Jeff said. He pulled a Pabst tallboy from his backpack and cracked it open.

Could you not do that, please? Welliger said. I feel like I've been very patient with you, sir. I've allowed you to drink liquor in my store, we've allowed you to go out and take that long smoke break, but this is too much. Please leave now.

Jeff sipped his beer and looked at Welliger. He said okay and started packing up. Murphy put up his hand, asked Jeff to sit back down.

Let me ask you something, Murphy said. So these are the men you served with?

Uh-huh.

I appreciate your service in the name of our freedom, French said. He reached out to shake Jeff's hand. Jeff took another sip.

Murphy pulled French and Welliger aside. All I heard was Welliger saying, I understand that, and, Yes but, and, Of course I respect his service, and Murphy told the two men to trust him. Then Murphy came back with a smile, Welliger sulking behind him.

I see what you're doing here, Murphy said. These men you drew, all looking down as if they're looming over something, maybe a corpse.

I don't know, Jeff said. Makes sense.

Our men in uniform, Murphy said, looking down on the broken bodies of our enemies. I like it. He doesn't have to draw Muhammed. None of us do. We don't even have to see him, just the brave men and women who will defeat his soldiers. They're all that matter.

He placed his hands on Jeff's shoulders and leaned in, whispered, *This is brilliant*, into Jeff's ear. Jeff took another sip of beer. French's lips stretched into a wide smile, and he grabbed Jeff's hand to shake it—he wasn't about to make the same mistake twice.

This is exactly what I'm talking about, French said. We don't care about your false prophet. We only care about the men who fight for us. Jesus Christ, this is genius.

Well, Murphy said, looks like we have a winner. Congratulations, Captain Logan.

Tell them about your comic, James, Jeff said.

Murphy told me he'd love to hear about it. He gave me his card and told me to send him an email, so we could talk in detail. I never heard back.

I think what James did took a lot of imagination, Jeff said. It's really cool what he was able to come up with. He should win the prize.

Yeah, Dennis the Menace said. Good work, bud.

Murphy said I definitely had a bright future and my heart swelled, even though I was still pissed that I lost. Bruce Murphy said I had a bright future.

Welliger said he agreed that I should be the winner, and told me I could come by next week for an interview, which felt great, even though I didn't even care about working there anymore. Fuck that store. According to my manager at Jack in the Box, the Chamber of Commerce was working on closing him down for this bullshit anyway.

Two weeks later, Jack in the Box let me go because of all the harassment they were getting.

A month later, Welliger made a public apology, saying he hosted the contest with the best of intentions and didn't mean to hurt anyone—not that it saved Shared Universe from becoming a Halloween outlet store again. French raged against him on the radio, called him a coward and a traitor. Then a couple dads from my school got caught trying to burn down a mosque, and French ended up losing his show.

And that was that. Jeff won the First, and only, Annual Draw Muhammed Contest, and I was Runner-Up. I had no idea how much harder my life was going to get after this—I just figured I was a loser before this and would probably have kept on being one after this anyway. I had no idea people were going to hate me the way they did because of some stupid contest I didn't even win. I even stopped reading and drawing comics because it hurt too much. I didn't think it would ruin my life the way it did. I just figured my life at that point was already in ruins, and that everything I was doing was going to help me escape, so I could return and reshape the world into something greater. But that was all a stupid fantasy—once something's ruined, it's always ruined. You can rebuild on top of the ruins, but you can never fix them. It's just something new, on top of something that was completely destroyed, and nothing you do can make you forget how badly everything got fucked.

Everyone gathered around Jeff and patted him on the back, told him how great it was, even Chavo, even Pissing Calvin Lady. They all marveled at his drawing, which really was beautiful. I don't think anyone else even saw how his hand shook when he raised that can of Pabst to his lips.

This Is the Afterlife

HE NIGHT before I left her, Miri told me the story of her mother, a story she'd told thousands of times, and now I wonder if she kept repeating it because I never knew how to respond. Here's the thing: Miri's mother was a crackpot. There's no other way of describing her. She'd passed away before Miri and I'd met, and it seems odd for me of all people to speak ill of the dead, but I was secretly relieved she'd wasted away before our paths crossed. According to her mother, the world as we knew it was to end on August 19, 1979, and I never knew if I was supposed to criticize the woman or feel pity for her. On that fateful day, the day of Man's reckoning with God, her mother had a stroke and fell into a coma. Miri was only fourteen years old at the time. She was sent to live with her aunt and uncle in San Diego, the place where she and I fell in love. The story always ended there—her age, her aunt and uncle, in the place we'd fallen in love.

Maybe she wanted me to relive the story each time, to really soak in the details, to find some kind of pattern. Or maybe she wanted to relive it herself because what she thought she'd understood, what I'd thought she'd understood, were actually things she knew nothing of. But maybe none of us actually understand any story that's been told— not in any collective sort of way, at any rate. Every time she relived her story, I relived her telling it, and there's a kingdom of difference between those two lives. After all, aren't the voices in our heads different from the ones spoken aloud to others? Maybe the stories we tell are just meant to stay voices in our heads, phantom languages that lose meaning once they travel from our minds to our lips.

I'm reminded of the time our daughter Nina came home from that rehab center in San Mateo—one year, four months, two weeks, three days ago—her hair stinking of cigarettes. Miri wanted to have a family night—just the three of us. But none of us could decide on a movie to watch, so Miri settled on *The Little Mermaid*, in spite of our reservations.

I still remember the first time you watched it, Miri told Nina. After it was over, you sighed and said, This is the most beautiful movie in the whole world!

Come on, Mama, Nina said. It's a movie about a girl who throws everything away for some dude because she wants to be independent, only to have her dad bail her out in the end. It's bullshit.

And as Nina came to her goddamn senses and tried to comfort her mother, as Miri turned away every time Nina tried to wrap her arms around her, all I could do was think about what Nina had said. It's just a movie about a girl who has to be saved by her father. I hadn't thought of it that way. And had I actually thought a little harder, perhaps I would've realized that Nina hated me because I'd bailed her out, that I'd pulled her out of school and sent her off to get cleaned up, that I'd only let her make her own mistakes up to a point. Why would any young girl in her situation want to watch a movie where the heroine is rescued by her father? I'd wanted to ask Nina if this was how she'd felt, but it never seemed right to ask this question out loud.

The morning before I left, I watched my soul escape my body. It wasn't painful in any way—I was actually watching the Niners play the Seahawks, which happened to be far more painful. My right palm opened up, and a tiny black bubble crowned from the hole in my hand. Then two tiny arms popped out, and two tiny hands pushed down against my palm, as this tiny man—who was my soul—wriggled his way out. By the time his feet touched the carpet, he was a full-sized thing who looked back at me before walking through the screen door and floating off to the sky. And with that, I was dead, even though it hadn't quite sunken in yet.

I walked over to Miri, who was in the kitchen reading the Sunday *Chronicle,* and told her I couldn't feel the right side of my body, so she rushed me to the Emergency Room. She cried the entire way there, and I tried to tell her I was fine.

Can you feel anything now? she asked, and I told her I couldn't, and I brushed the tears from her eyes and asked her if she wanted me to drive.

Are you fucking kidding me? she screamed.

I told her she was right, and I told her I was sorry—it was a stupid idea. I tried to tell her everything was okay, but I now realize everything probably wasn't okay. I'm sure in that moment, Miri was fourteen again, coming downstairs for breakfast to find her mother lying on the kitchen floor, the left side of her face melting downward as incoherent words bubbled from her lips. Her mother had spent all their money, sending it to the church, so the poor souls left behind could be taken care of in some small way. There were only two packets of instant oatmeal in the cupboard—one for each of them—their final meal before the Rapture. Her mother had made both packets in one bowl, in Miriam's bowl, Holly Hobby's faceless profile fading from the white plastic surface.

I'm going to be okay, I told her. Everything's fine.

She told me to stop saying everything was okay, and the right side of my body began tingling. I raised my right hand and wiggled my fingers, told Miri I could feel again, but she said we were going in anyway.

As the doctor ran tests, I thought about Nina, who'd called me on the way to the E.R. She told me she loved me, and I cried because it was everything I needed to hear. We hadn't gotten along since that night the school called, telling us she'd been found unconscious on the library staircase. They told us it was an overdose, that she'd been found lying in her own urine. They actually said that—lying in her own urine—why give that kind of detail over the phone?

We hadn't spoken much in the months since she'd come home from the rehab center. I hadn't forgiven her for blowing her scholarship, and Nina hadn't forgiven me for what she called my lack of empathy, and I hadn't forgiven her for saying that. I had plenty of empathy. She's my daughter—how could I not feel anything? I feel nothing but pain and sadness for her. I feel she's thrown away her future, for what? For drugs? I feel her addiction is an excuse, feel it's a crock of shit to go from Adderall to whatever it was she was snorting up her nose. I feel this is all a giant mess. And I feel love for her because I do love her. I feel these things now, as I did while sitting in the E.R., because I felt them when she said she loved me over the phone, and feelings don't go away when you die—they just spread out like water spilled on a glass surface.

The doctor, this young black man, told us the tests all came back negative—he didn't look stumped, which was very reassuring—and then asked me if I had been under any stress lately. Nina once told me you weren't supposed to point out someone's race the way I just did with that young doctor. I never understood what she was getting at, but she's always had a complicated relationship with race which I think she inherited from her mother. I'm sure it was much more complicated for them than it ever was for me. When Nina was a baby, people used to ask Miri where she'd adopted such a beautiful girl. And Nina spent her entire life being asked the question, What are you? Not, Who are you? but, What are you? as if she were some kind of thing, rather than a person, whose features were a point of curiosity—a Labradoodle. When she was in fourth grade, Miri had told Nina to say she was both Korean and Polish—not half-Korean, half-Polish—but that never stuck.

When we first moved into our home, when Miri was eight months pregnant with Nina, Fred Cable, the old man who lived across the street, came over to introduce himself. He pulled me aside and put his hand on my shoulder.

So you went and knocked up one of ours, did ya? he asked.

Miri and I fought that night because I'd laughed at his joke. She told me she didn't want to live in a world where her child was the butt of racist jokes, that I should have fought for both of them instead of laughing. But he was an old man with a cane who'd wanted to be friendly. And if I were to be completely honest with myself, it felt like a compliment at the time, as if he were welcoming me into a club that I hadn't belonged to until he'd acknowledged what I'd done. That all sounds very horrible now, and I never told Miri any of this. I simply told her she needed to get a sense of humor, and then did everything I could to keep her from crying.

At any rate, this young doctor was very professional and conscientious—he kept calling me Mr. Song when I told him to call me Jae—and I told him about Nina losing her Berkeley scholarship because of drugs and asked if that was stressful enough. And he said in a very even-tempered tone that it was very stressful, and he told me he was sorry, and thanked me for saying Berkeley instead of Cal, which apparently was a pet peeve of his. He was a nice young man, who just happened to be black, and he tried his best with the information he had.

Miri held my hand the entire drive home. I asked if I could turn on the radio, and she told me it was fine, as long as I wasn't going to rage at the post-game interviews. We settled on the Oldies station, which played Jackson Browne, and Fleetwood Mac, music Miri and I listened to when we were younger, and I wondered if the true purpose of nostalgia was to remind you that death was coming—that for many of us, it was already here. I remembered my nephew Aaron lying in the hospice bed, watching old *Popeye* cartoons, the way he looked at me when he said, I used to watch these all the time. Kids don't even watch these anymore.

He was only twenty-six years old. Miri loved him as if he were her own. He'd become an English teacher mainly because of her influence. I remember Miri, sitting next to me, while Popeye's arms became jackhammers, quoting some poem about looking at mighty works with despair, the two of them laughing. Aaron's eyes were wet, his lips dry and cracked. They never explained what they found so funny.

Remember when Oldies meant Elvis and "Rock Around the Clock"? I asked.

We're getting old, Jae, she said. We're the Oldies now. This is what inevitability sounds like.

It sounds like "Say You Love Me"?

She laughed, said it sounds exactly like Christine McVie, and squeezed my hand. You scared me back there, she said. What's going on?

I can't say, I said.

"Dancing Queen" began to play, and we talked about the home movie we made of Nina dancing to this song in her diaper, and we laughed. She told me that until we'd recorded that video, this song used to make her sad, and I thought, Of course it did. This is a song about death. I don't know how I knew that, but in that moment I knew: a woman watches a younger version of herself dancing in a club, realizes those days are gone, that there is only one possible outcome for her. "Dancing Queen" is a ghost story, but who is the ghost—the young dancer or the older woman? I need to understand.

What are you thinking about? Miri asked.

Remember when Nina came back from the dentist and kept saying, I used to be dead. I used to be dead, Mama!

When Nina was five, a new tooth began growing behind a baby tooth, so we were asked to bring her in to have the tooth pulled. It was a children's dentist downtown, more Disneyland than dentist's office. The waiting room was a giant play area. Off in the back corner, a small private theater showed *The Rescuers Down Under* on a projection screen.

As we signed her in, Nina immediately ran to an empty Nintendo 64 station and began playing *Mario Kart*. Children ran and shouted and laughed throughout the expansive waiting area. A young boy around Nina's age sat in a corner, slamming Hello Kitty's skull with a toy hammer, over and over and over.

They finally called Nina's name, and we took her little hands, and the assistant led us down a long hallway in the back. As we got closer and closer to the door, we could hear the children sobbing and screaming, the shrieking drills and crackling suction of the saliva ejectors. Nina clutched Miri's hand and buried her face into Miri's thigh, whimpered as the children around us cried No, over and over and over.

We came to a tiny, antiseptic room with a dentist's chair. The first things I noticed were the straps on the armrests, the long belt that dangled on the floor. Miri took a seat on a stool, pulled Nina onto her lap, tried to ignore the tormented children in the other rooms.

On the drive home, Nina clutched her Little Mermaid doll, drugged out of her mind. Every time Miri asked if she was feeling okay, she told us she used to be dead.

How're you feeling, sweetie?

I used to be dead.

Should we have tater tots with dinner?

I used to be dead.

Why are you saying that, baby?

I used to be dead, Mama.

Miri didn't think this was as funny as I did, frantically asking her to stop even though Nina couldn't help herself. The last time I'd thought about this incident was after the overdose, when Nina told us she was convinced she'd died on those library staircases.

I died, Mama. Right there on those stairs. As I looked down through the railing, I could see the sun floating beneath me.

And I thought about the trip to the dentist, how her declarations of death had made her mother cry, and became furious. I told her it

149

was the tiling that formed a mosaic of the sun. She'd seen it hundreds of times. Nothing was different, except her brain was fried from the drugs she never should have taken in the first place. And she told me she knew, and we wouldn't speak again for weeks.

Goddammit, Jae, Miriam said. Why are you bringing that up? I still have waking nightmares about her saying that. I used to be dead, Mama. I used to be dead. It's not funny.

I'm sorry, I said. Just something that came to mind.

Miriam turned down the volume so we were no longer really listening to Abba. It felt more like eavesdropping.

You know what that dentist reminded me of? Miri asked. Pleasure Island from Pinocchio, where all those kids were trapped and turned into donkeys. All those kids playing video games, watching cartoons, playing Legos—they had no idea what they were in for in the back with those drills and gas masks.

Waking nightmares, she called them. How could I ever tell her what was happening to me? None of it would make sense even if I could.

It's just cruel, she said.

You're right, I said. Getting kids riled up like that, and then taking them to a roomful of drills. I hadn't thought of it that way.

Now I'm sad.

Let's not think about it anymore, I said. Let's remember Nina when she didn't used to be dead, when she shimmied in her diaper to this song.

And I turned up the volume and tried to smile. Who's the ghost, Miri? Is it me or is it you? I'm still not sure.

My soul spoke to me as I stepped out of the car, and into the garage. I knew it was my soul because it sounded like the voice in my head—just a personification of words and images. I'll never forget that moment, actually hearing the voice inside my head. It sounded nothing like the spoken words vibrating through my skull, or the one vibrating in another's ears—simply words forming in my head and rolling like smoke in a bottle. My soul spoke to me in Korean. The last time I'd even spoken Korean was three years ago at AT&T Park, in the Giants Dugout Store, as a translator for a tourist from Daejeon. I can't even remember the last time I dreamt in Korean. Do I have random thoughts in Korean? My childhood flashbacks—did the voice translate those into English or did subtitles form in my head and dissipate into the core of my eardrum? This was far more unsettling than the fact my wayward soul was calling to me—of course my soul would call to me. What else would it do?

It told me I had to leave, that I had to get in my car and drive. When I asked where I had to go, it told me I had to drive. It didn't answer when I asked why we were speaking in Korean, if we were actually speaking Korean. Miri leaned into my back, locked her fingers around my waist, rested her chin on my shoulder.

Dureibu, I said.

What was that?

That's drive in Korean.

Oh, she laughed. English bastardization.

I don't know. Maybe it's a Korean bastardization.

Miri kissed my neck and unlocked her fingers. She took my hand and said we should get inside, asked me if I wanted anything to eat.

Un jun hada, I said.

What does that mean?

Same thing.

Why are you saying drive in Korean?

I don't know. I'm just glad to be home. Can we just sit around as a family tonight? Maybe we can order pizza, watch a movie.

She gave me a hug and said we could do anything I wanted. We went inside. I took off my shoes. We never took off our shoes.

I convinced Nina we should watch *The Little Mermaid* as a family, convinced her to suggest it. The voice kept telling me to drive, and I told it, Later, that I was busy, and Nina kept asking if I was feeling okay, that I looked flustered, and I did my best not to snap at her.

Look, Dad, she said, this whole thing has me thinking about how much I fucked everything up.

What whole thing? I asked.

Jesus Christ, you just got out of the hospital, remember? Seriously, are you okay right now?

Un jun hada, the voice said. Then, *Dureibu*. I told Nina I was fine.

Well, anyway, I just want you to know I'm sorry about everything. I swear I never wanted to disappoint you.

I told her I wasn't disappointed in her, even though I was. Lying just felt like the right thing to do—it felt good. But part of me still wondered if I was supposed to be honest with her. Maybe I was supposed to tell her she'd let us all down. Maybe I was supposed to tell her how angry I was. Maybe I was supposed to tell her not to throw her life away, not to waste it the way she had been since dropping out. Maybe I was supposed to tell her I didn't bust my ass so that she could work part-time at the JC Penney make up counter.

But lying felt right. She held me and sobbed—it felt right.

These past few months, she said, I felt like a ghost. Like you guys knew I was dead, but humored me because you loved me enough to treat me like I belonged here. I'm sure that doesn't make any sense.

Remember that Thanksgiving when Mama and I argued whether light was a wave or a particle?

Yeah, she said. I told you it was both and you got mad because it supposedly didn't make sense.

Wave-particle duality, she'd called it at the time. Something to do with Schrödinger and Einstein, Newton and some other person whose name escapes me—she'd even begun drawing equations and formulas on a napkin, as if that would somehow make sense to us. I wasn't angry that it didn't make any sense—it didn't—I was angry because she'd told Miri and me we were both wrong. As brilliant as she was, she couldn't see we were both right. Nina's eyes narrowed, and she leaned in as if she were near-sighted.

Dad, why are you thinking about that right now?

Because that didn't make sense, I said. Waves and particles? I don't understand those things. But what you just said right now, I completely understand. I understand what you're saying perfectly. Promise me you'll never forget that.

I crawled into bed with my wife one last time, held her for one last time. I rested my cheek against the back of her head and closed my eyes, and for the last time I tried to ignore the voice. When I left later that night, I made sure not to disturb her—no goodbye kiss, no longing last look from the threshold.

What are you thinking? she asked.

The Little Mermaid, I said. She chose to stay on land, instead of going home to her family. Doesn't that make you a little sad?

Jesus Christ, Jae. Don't you ruin this memory the way your daughter did the last time.

I told her I was sorry, began to cry. She asked what was wrong, and I told her I didn't really know, that I just didn't want to lose anyone. She cried and told me she wasn't going anywhere, that we were always going to be together.

I'm sorry for freaking out today, she said. I'm sure that didn't help. I just thought maybe you were having a stroke, and I thought I was going to lose you the way I lost my mom.

I told her I knew, and she told me again of August 19, 1979, because she couldn't help herself. Christ was to return to Earth that day, and take the Saved up to heaven, leaving the rest of us to suffer fire and brimstone, plagues upon the earth, until the world finally ended five months later. Her mother began spending all their money on resources for the church—they weren't going to need the money where they were going—and because of this, they were to be evicted from their home three days before the stroke.

But the world didn't end, she said. For anyone else that is.

Maybe it did, the voice whispered in Korean.

What was that?

Oh, I said maybe it did.

Well it didn't, and I'm glad. I remember her funeral, all these people gathered in the chapel paying their respects, and the whole time I knew they were judging her. I knew they were laughing at her, the entire funeral home gloating because she'd told them they were all going to burn. What a fucking waste her life was.

But what if it did? I said. What if she was right? What if the world did end, and we're the ones left behind?

She pulled me in, kissed me, and we made love for the last time, and the voice told me to drive—*Dureibu, Un jun hada,* in succession, at the same time, vibrating through my skull, dissipating into the core of my eardrum.

Jeff Chon is the author of the novel *Hashtag Good Guy With a Gun* (Sagging Meniscus, 2021).